C. J. Hribal

MATTY'S HEART

MATTY'S HEART

DISCARDED

C. J. Hribal

Drawings by Tracy Turner

Minnesota Voices Project #20

New Rivers Press 1984

Copyright © 1984 by C. J. Hribal and Tracy Turner
Library of Congress Catalog Card Number: 84-061823
ISBN: 0-89823-057-8
All rights reserved
Book Design: Daren Sinsheimer and C. W. Truesdale
Typesetting: Peregrine Cold Type

Grateful acknowledgement for suggestions and support is made to: Tom Townfley and Ron Block, Tobias Wolff and Raymond Carver, C. W. Truesdale, and the extended Hribal-Kornilowizc family. Some places in this book are real, though their geography has been changed. Every character is fictitious. "Matty's Heart" was a finalist in the 1984 Minnesota Short Story Project. "Stephers" was one of eight finalists in the 1984 *Mademoiselle* Short Fiction Competition.

Matty's Heart has been published with the aid of grant support from the Jerome Foundation, the Dayton Hudson Foundation (with funds provided by B. Dalton, Bookseller), The First Bank System Foundation, the United Arts Fund (with funds provided in part by the McKnight Foundation), and the Metropolitan Regional Arts Council (with funds appropriated by the Minnesota State Legislature).

New Rivers Press books are distributed by:

    Small Press Distribution, Inc.   Bookslinger
    1784 Shattuck Ave.   213 East 4th St.
    Berkeley, CA 94709   St. Paul, MN 55101

Matty's Heart has been manufactured in the United States of America for New Rivers Press, Inc. (C. W. Truesdale, editor/publisher), 1602 Selby Ave., St. Paul, MN 55104 in a first edition of 1000 copies.

To Krystyna

MATTY'S HEART

Matty's Heart, 9

Stephers, 34

Fixing Cars and Oklahoma, 46

3-D, 51

Lake Poygan and the Politics of Departure, 57

The Night of the Spoon, 65

Kitchens, 77

Biographical Notes, 101

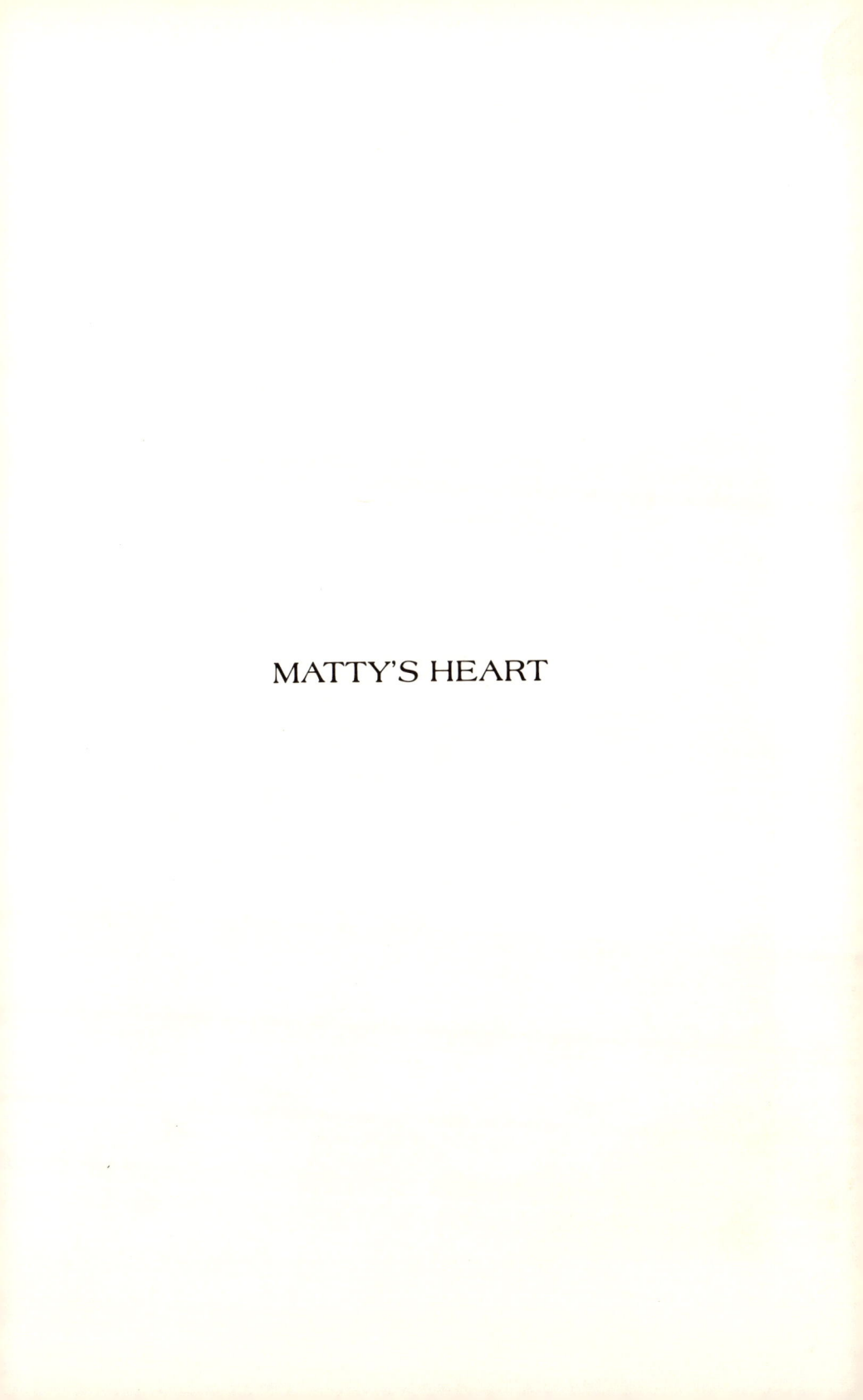

MATTY'S HEART

MATTY'S HEART

I've done things from necessity that hurt others just to hear. But that's changed now and for twenty-one years I've been Augsbury's town clerk, working in the back of the town hall, in an office at the end of the short corridor which has the police station on one side and the volunteer fire department on the other.

I don't like my position here, tucked away from everything but paperwork. Augsbury has no mayor. It's ruled by a town board consisting of Frank Buss, of Buss's Foods, Joe Morley of Morley Insurance, and Art Butler, Dick Bradka and Henry Dorffman, all farmers. The board drinks beer two Wednesdays a month and I do the work. Leona Griemerts is my assistant, a plowhorse of a woman capable of everything but independent thought.

We're doing tax assessments. Augsbury Township has a tad over 5000 people (1700 in town proper), and we have 1400 envelopes to stuff, address, and mail. I'm a fifty-seven-year-old postal machine and Leona, thirteen years my junior, has aspirations to be what I'm tired of being.

I give Leona a look, she puts her emery board back in her purse, flips to M in the tax records and we set to. Alice Mumphrey owes one hundred and thirty-seven dollars; John Mumster four hundred and thirteen. All the while Leona rattles on. Chatters about her garden, planned, her children, unplanned, and her husband, whose lack of plans upsets her. What is there in the reel of sound that keeps her at it?

"You know, Matty, Howard hasn't come home from Poachers' lately till nearly closing. It used to be he'd go down there once a week, maybe twice, and have a few. I didn't mind that. Let them have it out of them, I say. A little here and there and they feel they have free rein. But that's the problem. They really get to thinking it. Howard's there nearly every night now after milking. And yesterday he didn't get up till half past eight. He's beginning to be like your Ben—"

Your Ben. As if I ever owned him.

"—And have you heard anymore from Frankie? It must break your heart.

9

Myself, I couldn't believe it when he up and ran off like that. What are those kids thinking of, anyway? Is it true he went to Australia and ate dog meat?"

I'm a woman with seven children, one of them dead and only three of them truly whole. Matthew is the oldest. He and his wife and two children live in Maine. He left here when he was twenty-seven and fishes for lobster now outside Kennebunkport. Amanda, my second, has three little ones and a solid husband. Their farm is clean and well-run. One hundred and sixty-seven cows, three hundred and twelve acres, big for around here, and three hired hands. Amanda married smart, but that's all I'll say for her. She treats her children badly and misused children become misshapened adults. Even with children treated fairly, there's so much to go wrong. I pray against such things, but, Lord, what's happened. Ben was already dead inside two years ago, but Rupert. My God, Rupert.

Rupert was after Amanda and before Frankie. Those first four were quick. I don't remember early on not being pregnant, not being ill, not lacking strength, my blood going off to someplace inside me where it stayed but I couldn't use it. Rupert was the hardest. My third child and thirty-two hours of labor. And even then a C-section. Doc Meyer split me open like a chicken breast.

After Frankie, it was two and a half years to Isabel, then that again to Rose and that again to Fred. I joked to Ben he was getting slower. He knew he was dying all that while and didn't think my joke funny. I saw him dying, too, which is why I wanted his children. I wanted pieces of him, of us, to last longer than we did. But except for Matthew and Isabel and Fred, Fred, our last, our love child, the closest to Matthew in everything but age, all of them came out broken, or broke quickly afterwards. I wanted to blame Ben, as if his seed was not only slow, it was weak.

It wasn't, of course. I only thought that way because cancer was in him like chokeweed already and I wanted to blame everything on that. I don't begrudge him the drinking later, either, though others have, Leona among them. When Ben died there was nothing in him, he was hollowed, a dry gourd.

"You know what Howard does now, don't you? He tells them at Poachers' to say he's over at the Silver Dollar and at the Silver Dollar they say he's at Utke's. Utke's says he's on his way home. He thinks he's fooling me, got me running around on the phone. He has quite a laugh at it with his friends, I'm sure. 'Got the missus on the run, now,' he'll be saying. I can just see it. But it's not like I don't know he's at Poachers' the whole while. And he knows I know it. He's not fooling me a bit. Honestly, he's like your Frankie was, only at least Howard eventually comes home. You ever figure out what got into Frankie anyway?"

What got into Frankie: everything that's in Frankie was there in the beginning. He was born with no connection to this life. All babies' eyes are born unfocused, but his were already on the distance. His faith gone there, too, when he was old enough to reason faith. But the faith he reasoned was not a faith I'd wanted for him, and the only thing Ben taught him was hard work. Ben taught work to all his sons. "The women are up to you," he said. "The boys are mine." Rupert was never strong enough to work as Ben wanted. Ben cast him off as only fit for women's work, but Ben really couldn't stand for that, either, so Rupert took over the chores in between—the outside women's work—gathering eggs, cleaning the coops, forking hay into the stalls, tending vegetables.

Matthew left to get married, to do more work, only to do it someplace else. It bothered Ben that Matt left like that, but when Matt got his own boat after three years of working for somebody else, Ben accepted it. The real problems were with Frankie. Frankie didn't break to anybody, and that was what Ben expected from his sons, that they break like draft animals in their father's service, and for Frankie not doing such, for Frankie being as strong as his own father, Ben hated him. I remember Ben once ordering Frankie to manure the field between the creek and the back hill. It was a Saturday, the sun had already set, and Frankie had friends waiting at Blackie's. They were going night fishing on the Wolf. The job would take close to three hours in the dark. "Fuck off, old man," Frankie said, and drove the pickup to town, two rods and the tackle box in the back. Frankie was sixteen then.

I'm getting ahead of Leona so I tell her I'll get the coffee. We don't have our own pot; we have to share with Clayton Jones and his two deputies, and they keep the coffee in their office. The board laughed the last time I tried getting a pot for back in our corner of the world. Joe Morley thought it was nice how we didn't have to go to the fire station next door and use their urn. Thirty dollars for a coffee maker was too much, how could they justify that expense when there was a perfectly good pot just down the hall? Clayton tells me at least I don't have to make it; he has Bud Willers, his skinny-faced deputy, do that. Bud Willers is only one of two people I know who can scorch coffee without working at it. But the men here have a strange notion of protocol. To show I'm equal to them, they make burned coffee for me.

I rinse out the dust in Leona's and my mugs and add cream to Leona's. Then about three teaspoons of sugar. Mine's black. Leona makes up for everything she didn't have when she was a girl by adding three times what she needs now. She's getting doughy. All her edges have gone soft but she shrugs her shoulders when I ask her about exercise as if such a question were beyond her power to answer.

I pinch my own forearm, my bicep—hickory staves and baling wire, as always. At one time, when thirty was a new age to me, I'd let myself go soft like Leona. My hips swelled like dinner muffins. I wore paisley housecoats, hoping the pattern would blend out the bulk. Somedays I'd eat nonstop—cold fried chicken while I did the dishes, soap suds on the ends of the chicken legs. I wouldn't even rinse my hands. After the first flurry of children were up, dressed, and on to school, I'd sit the morning through eating cherry cobbler and drinking coffee or apple juice. I'd spend three hours making doughnuts and eat through lunch. Ben'd slap my thigh when he'd come in for noon. He didn't say anything about the softness, but I guess he liked it. He'd pick up a doughnut and say,

"These just for you, or me, too?" He'd have a doughnut and milk and stew, then clap on his cap and head back to the barn or a side field. He favored De Kalb corn caps then ("The wings on the cob are gonna take me clear to heaven, despite myself," he said), but later, when he got sick and the corn cob angel wings looked strangely prophetic, he took to wearing chemical caps—Dinaflox or Tuff-E-Nuff Wormite—as if they would work on his insides the way they did the parasites on the corn stalks. And later still, he wore a Monroe Shock Absorber cap, the visor grease-broken and the rim dark with sweat. His caps were his philosophy, his advertisements of belief. It was during his later De Kalb days I got fat.

It seems like everything happens at once, but that's not true. There is an order to things, but the time is now distant enought that my sense of the sequence is confused. I can't remember if he got sick first, or if he changed caps first, but right after that I ran for the clerk job, won (by default), and my body got hard again.

Behind me the glass door swings open. I look to see if it's Clayton or Bud, both of whom stop in during the day for coffee to go with the sweet roll they buy at Verhagen's. People would talk if they actually had the coffee and sweet roll at Verhagen's, so they come back here to do the paperwork, which is to say they eat a jelly long john and read yesterday's *Post Crescent*.

But it's neither Clayton nor Bud. It's Cecil Alt. Cecil Jr., actually. The elder Alt's been dead six months. Ben and Cecil were partners in the growth gone crazy that took them both. They had different ways of dying, though. Over the years Ben folded in on himself, like a cardboard box left out in the rain. Cecil became a health nut. Ate measured amounts of food, abstained from anything not specifically mentioned in his book, and went twice a month down to Oshkosh for acupuncture. Some say it took his pain away better than any vitamin or medicine he took, others say it let the air out of him like a tack does to a bicycle tire so he just didn't have anything left in him to feel. Whatever, it didn't cure him. He died a week before Ben.

Cecil Jr.'s in his mid-thirties now. His hair is wild and thin. He started going bald when he was sixteen, and now on each side of his high forehead big rounds of scalp show as if someone had traced goose egg shapes over his head and cut them out. He's wearing what he always wears—a plaid orange and green sport shirt with double breast pockets, and Lee jeans, baggy in the rear so it looks as if he has no behind. He's also got on a hunting vest.

"Hello, Cecil." I'm stirring Leona's coffee. Her sugar takes a minute or two to dissolve.

Cecil's out of breath. "Anybody here?"

"Leona."

"Not Jones? Or Bud?"

"Just us."

Cecil pushes his hair back. It's pretty long to be in his eyes, considering the trip it takes to fall forward. He's worn it like that since he came back to town. He left about the same time as Frankie, but he came two days later. Cecil didn't have the right kind of feet.

"I'll be right back," Cecil says.

I take the coffee to Leona.

"I nearly caught up with you," she says. She's still a half-dozen envelopes behind me. A *McCall's* is open on top of the ledger. I flip it closed. Leona shrugs.

"Good coffee." She says that every morning, though what she's drinking isn't remotely related to coffee.

Cecil's back. I watch him poke his head into the police office, then he comes striding back to us. He's carrying a doublebarrel twelve gauge and a box of shells.

"Season's not open till September, Cecil. And Tom won't sell you the license till June." Sefert's Coast to Coast Hardware Store takes care of the hunting and fishing licenses. We used to, but it makes more sense for Tom to do it, since they all go over there for shells, guns and baitboxes anyway.

"Not here for the hunting." Cecil motions us away from the table. We move. Cecil tucks the gun against his shoulder and blasts the table in half. Splinters of linoleum and bits of paper leap away from the table as if detonated. Leona shrieks.

Cecil puts the box of shells on the other table and reloads the one barrel. He turns around and fires both barrels down the hall. Glass shatters and metal screams. Footsteps come running—the fire station. They run out their garage doors and gather in front of the wreckage. Cecil's reloaded.

"Christ," one of them says. It sounds like Pete Wilson. I can't tell because Cecil's blocking my view.

"Nobody comes in!" Cecil yells at them. "I got women back here."

My gut hurts as if stricken. Something foul-smelling washes up from my stomach. I want to throw up but I won't. It's like when I stand up with a fever and my eyes are packed with wet cotton and my vision is gone. Everything normal is out of my head. I steady myself with a hand on the destroyed table. One side of the tax ledger is blown to bits. Leona has sat down on a wooden folding chair. I hear her urine run in a dribbling stream from a gap between two slats. My ears are still ringing and my nose is filled with the smells of gunpowder and piss.

"Who's that? Who's in there?" The voice is Frank Spivey's. He works the late shift at the wire works and sleeps through the morning at the fire station. Then he eats lunch at Blackie's and goes home for a few hours. He lives alone at the trailer court.

"I got two women," Cecil calls. "I got Leona Griemerts and Matty Keillor."

"Who are you?" Frank says.

I can't see, but I'd guess Frank is away from the door by now. Maybe one hand touches the twisted remainder of the stainless steel and double-paned Weatherall, but I doubt if he's any closer.

"Cecil Alt."

"Cecil? Cecil's dead."

13

"I'm his boy."

"Young Cecil? What the hell you doing with a gun?"

I pull the other folding chair and sit down with my hands folded together in my lap. I think how if I had gone through most of my life being Young Cecil, or Cecil's boy, or Junior, perhaps I'd carry around a shotgun, too. But then I think I've been Ben Keillor's wife for as long as I've been anything, and though it was never the way I thought of myself, even when I was referred to only in that way, I was never tempted to violence.

Cecil is leaning forward, like a pointer, his gun pulled close to his stomach. If someone yelled, "Pull!" I'd expect him to swing and fire. I bow my head and begin to pray.

Cars screech outside, one and then another. I get up. It's Jones and Willers, Willers' front bumper touching Jones' back bumper. They get out, walk across the doorway. Cecil is standing next to me, watching them. He's still holding the gun at his hip. Jones squints inside, but it's a lot darker in here than it is out there, and if he sees anything at all it's just dark figures.

"Move your cars!" Frank says. "For God's sake, move your cars."

"That you, Cecil?" Jones shouts. "That you in there?" Jones takes a step forward. His body and head are shaped like eggs—bottom-heavy and round, one stacked on the other. Except for a fringe of strange orange hair, clipped to nubbins, Jones is bald. His face is flushed.

"You're not gonna shoot now, are you, Cecil?"

The first shot goes over their heads. Jones dives one way, Willers another. I can't see them anymore. Cecil takes out the one shell he's fired and takes out the other bullet, too. He reloads with two green plastic shells. The air explodes. And again. The whole back end of Jones' car is peppered with shot, the tire's flat. The paint's flaked off in rough round holes. Willers' front is the same. Cecil reloads. Two more KAROOMS. My ears ring. Jones' rear window bursts and something is leaking from under the hood of Willers' car. Cecil's switched back to slugs.

From the back of his vest he takes a bottle of Jack Daniels. He breaks the seal and gulps down a fair amount, enough so that bubbles of air travel up through the bottle.

"Who's all in there with him?" Jones shrieks.

"Leona and Matty."

"Christ." Jones' swearing is a bad sign, he won't swear unless things are getting away from him. In a crisis he has to work very hard to not go to pieces. I imagine him rubbing his pate, hoping to rub an idea into his head with his fingers. "All right, let me think," he says.

He sounds calmer now. I can't tell if it's true calm or put-on calm. Jones has been known in the past to get antsy and do stupid things. Like the time the motorcycle gang came up from Milwaukee and started raising hell at Poachers' Inn. Jones called them all outside. A small crowd gathered. The six bikers came out still holding their beers. I think they were genuinely interested in seeing what this small marble-bellied figure intended to do. Jones asked them to leave town, they were bothering people. "Bothering people? Who's bothered? Anybody bothered? Are you bothered, ma'am?" one of them asked old Mrs. Harris. They all grinned. Another swilled beer around in his glass until some sloshed onto Jones' pants. The biker apologized profusely and everybody laughed, the crowd nervously, the bikers hysterically. Jones lost it and pulled his gun. Something got said and he fired a warning shot in the air. Only he was standing under a streetlight and glass from the light he shot out rained down on him and some of the crowd. Two people needed stitches.

So I strain now to hear Jones. I have a bad feeling that he's going to get people hurt for no other reason than his inability to act sensibly.

"First things first," Jones says. "Frank, you and Pete go around back and get out the road block signs. We can't have somebody getting shot accidently. I'll stay here and make sure no one crosses in front of the door. Bud, come here. You there, stand back. You, too, Mrs. Nelson."

I try to picture the crowd that must be gathering. It's my connection to composure, to imagine myself out there with them. Standing next to Irene Nelson, maybe, who's probably on the edge of the circle with her walker, wondering why she can't get through to the grocery store. Or I'd be like Celia Wandtke, offering assistance. Celia's home on leave from the Air Force, where she's a traffic MP, to convince her half-sister, Wanda, to go into the military after high school. Mary, Celia's mother, told me this when she called up earlier this week to ask about her water bill. Celia had found opportunity in the Air Force, Mary said, and Wanda needed something like that. Mary wasn't Wanda's mother. Wanda was the product of one of her father's forays into the Oneida Indian Reservation. Wanda's mother hadn't wanted the baby after she found out its father was a married man with a child of his own to support, not that Henry Wandtke did much of that anyway. She'd come into town to place Wanda on Henry's doorstep. She rang the bell and waited. She hand-delivered her baby to its father. She also gave Henry Wandtke a receipt for the child and had some words of advice for Mary. "I'd cut off his cock," the woman said, "and that would only be partial payment for what he's done to both of us." Celia, eight, has been standing behind her parents when all this was said. Growing up with that has been hard for her. It's been a nightmare for Mary and Wanda.

Other people I guess I'd see there: Dave Kapp, the salesclerk at the Party Port, who probably sold the Jack Daniels to Cecil, and whose pregnant girlfriend, Shelly Farber, had come in this morning to find out what she needed to do about getting married. Dave will be wondering if Shelly is still in here and asking everyone who doesn't know. Others: Tom and Marcy Sefert, from the hardware store; Joe Morley, whose company insures the ruined police cars; Louise Garret, the chiropractor on Main Street who once charged $250 to look at Ben and poked his back and sides for two hours; Milly Thompson, who visits me regularly on Thursdays to get a new recipe but never gets them right (so her husband tells me), and who, if I were to die, would mourn the passing of my rhubarb pie more than my own passing.

Porter Atwood would be out there, too, if he's in town today. Porter would come up to me, dressed in a blue denim leisure suit and say how he sees me so rarely these days and why is that now? Porter is the smooth-talking real estate agent and auctioneer who comes by every spring asking if Ben wants to sell any of the back woodlot. Porter has a vision of himself as being smarter than all the local yokels, and maybe he is. What Porter does is catch farmers at lean times and talk them up, sound real magnanimous in baling them out with ready cash. All you have to do is sell a few measly acres here and there. Porter then divides them up and sells each fraction of an acre to city people who want to live in the country. Eventually every back field Porter gets looks like a new subdivision, crammed full of cracker-box houses for people who want to get away from it all. I shudder to think what he'll do to our place. Ben hated Porter, would've shot him outright on general principle, but that didn't stop me from making a fool of myself with him.

Nonetheless, the only person I'm absolutely sure is out there is Byron Joe Gunther. Byron Joe, whose stomach is just a tad smaller than a lye cauldron, whose arms are twice as big as any other man's, whose massive shoulders, chest and gut rest on spindly legs as if all the matter had been sucked from his calves and thighs and went into that bloated fleshy mound of gut with its belly-button countersunk three inches. His face is red and bullet-shaped. His eyes are slits and long jowls hang into a second chin and part of a third. Byron Joe is in his mid-thirties and crushes tin beer cans with one hand. He never works that I can see, except infrequently as the self-appointed bouncer at Poachers', but he always has money and even Jones keeps his distance. It was Byron Joe who eventually got the bikers to leave. He told them they were wasting their time on chicken shits. Byron Joe is a drunken bear on the streets of Augsbury, and no one dares say boo. He's been in here twice, surly both times, pawing, with fingers that look like two of mine welded together, through papers and asking questions he had no right to get answers to. I threw him out both times, politely, once with Jones' help, and I'm sure right now Byron Joe has flipped the tab of another Budweiser and is grinning. If I were out there he'd grin over whoever was trapped back here. He'd wink at me as if we shared a secret.

"What kind of underwear an old woman like you got on these hot days?" he asked the last time he was in.

I didn't answer.

"They still get wet when a man of bulk come by? That still get you hot?" Both paws came down on the desk top. He leaned forward, his breath stale, his eyes glossy. I hammered on the wall with my desk stapler. It was enough to get Jones' attention. He ushered Byron out, gesturing with his hands as if shooing a stray bull.

I've never seen Byron all the way out of control. I wonder if I would have if Jones hadn't been a cinder block away.

Cecil motions for me to get him a folding chair. I pick up mine. He arranges it so he's facing the door, just a lean away from firing straight down the corridor. He has a pull from his bottle, then sets that between his feet. It doesn't look like I'm going to get the quick drunken stupor I was praying for. Redemption is still two-thirds of a bottle away.

I think about redemption. Not the eternal one, which isn't something I'm prepared for, but immediate salvation. My rescue, such as it will be. Jones will deliver me to Herbert Tessen, the foreman at the wire works. He's probably outside right now, having heard the commotion on his way home for lunch. I can see him standing behind a barricade, his hands in his pockets, his shoulders pulled in toward his chin, finding out from Jones exactly what's happened to his beloved. Me.

Herb's is a one-sided love that chugs ahead despite my complete lack of interest. It's not even love, either. If it were I might not avoid him so much. Herb Tessen got widowed four years ago and when it was apparent Ben was going to die soon he came over and proposed the likelihood of us getting together. His argument was based on nothing save his notion that the proper way for people to be was coupled and when halves were missing the remedy was to find another half. You could worry about the fit later. "That's something we can hammer into shape after the fact," he said, the fact being our nuptials. Ben wasn't even dead yet.

What was worse was that since he'd thought this out, to himself, at least, he'd considered the bond to be there already. I just had to be made aware of it. His idea was to ask me to his church (this, at least, was early December, a full month after I'd buried Ben) and then have breakfast. He saw no need to pitch everything all at once: wills, property, bank accounts. You had to start with the simplest things, he said, dousing his wheat pancakes in syrup: would I convert from Catholicism to Missouri Synod Lutheran for him? He assured me if it was the other way around, me proposing to him, he'd do the same for me.

He said he was even willing to take on Rose. "That crippled daughter of yours," was how he put it. Herbert Tessen explained this to me with an air of resignation, Rose being a liability, a twisted half, never to be made whole, that he was accepting for my sake, seeing as how the operations, the praying to God, the novenas, none of it had worked.

He's cursing Cecil Alt right now. That crazed boy, Herbert's thinking, that crazed boy is right now in there with a shotgun and Matty. My Matty.

I imagine Herbert worrying about what will happen because of Cecil and his shotgun. I might, in some crazy female way, mix up his intentions with those of Cecil Alt, I might lump him in that same category, lump him in with all the other men who are crazy and blind and chasing just one thing. I might back off from his proposal entirely, thinking God was punishing me for having such thoughts as to marry outside my faith, even though my faith was a pack of papal lies. He knows how women can be. Alma, his first wife, had that streak in her, a private philosophy that guided her clear through any and all obstacles. He confided to me it'd been hell living with her. He assumes I'm different.

Cecil swivels towards us.

"I can't be watching the two of you," he says. He motions at Leona with the barrel. "Get out of here."

"I can't," Leona says. "I mean, not right away." Leona's been working furiously with her handkerchief. She continues to wipe the dark spot on her puff blue skirt. "I'll just be a minute," she says. "Maybe fifteen."

Cecil shakes his head.

"I can't just yet," Leona says. "I'll be a laughingstock."

"I could blow your head off as easy as sitting here."

Leona dabs twice more, but she's already moving. She takes her purse and she's gone, tossing a "Take care, Matty" back at me from the door as if this were the end of a Tupperware Party. I'd hate her furiously except I'd go just the same if it were me.

I want to ask Cecil if he'd really have shot her, but I'm afraid of the answer. He has another swig of the Jack and pats time on his thighs. I try to imagine the tune. What song would have Cecil counting time on his thighs? And from what thing to what thing does his mind leap? What strage logic has taken him farther afield than even Byron Joe Gunther? Byron Joe, who's been on a short fuse as long as he's been padding up and down Main and Roosevelt, going from the bowling alley to the Party Port to the DX to Poachers' to Blackie's Cafe to the canning company, where he and Bob Notlinger, the sanitation foreman, split an afternoon six-pack ("a hydraulic lunch" to Ben).

Cecil and Byron Joe and Frankie. What have we done that our children have come to this?

Frankie left the week after Cecil tried to enlist and was turned down. Before he went to Chicago, Cecil's parents had a party for him, a little ceremony at their place. About thirty people, including Ben and me. Cecil Jr. and Sr. showed off the Edsels they'd collected. They had eleven at the time—a rainbow of Edsels, from solid blacks and gunmetal blues to two-toned forest and pastel green. That green one was the family car. Eventually there were twenty-five Edsels at the Alt place, scattered about like windfall apples. Fourteen ran, the rest were cannibalized for parts. The elder Alt took me for a ride in the green and white Edsel that day. He was always taking people—people he knew and could trust—for rides in his green and white Edsel. It was his way of conversing. He'd drive and drive, going nowhere in particular ("meandering about" Ben said), and about when you thought he wasn't going to say anything, though you knew he wanted to, he'd shift his toothpick—he grabbed handfuls of the mint ones on his infrequent dinners out—and say what it was he felt needed saying. Not more or less.

On that day he told me, "I'm proud he's my son, Matty. Real proud. He ain't a coward," he said, looking at me sideways, as if he already knew what it was Frankie was going to do, but of course he couldn't. "But I'm afraid of losing him as my son. Parts of him I call my own are going to get changed. I know what happens in a war. Craziness. They go hog-wild. We won't be people he'll recognize when he comes back. And I won't recognize him. What he'll learn won't be things I'd want him learning."

I could say nothing to him he didn't already know. I told him to think about when Cecil would come home, not about now, when he's going. And Cecil Sr. said, "That's what I am thinking about."

As it turned out, it didn't matter. Cecil was back two days after he left, flat feet and a heart murmur the grounds for rejection.

Cecil stands upright so fiercely the chair clatters to the floor behind him. I start, heart leaping and stopping high in my chest, from where I've been cleaning up Leona's chair and the floor around it with paper toweling and Windex gotten from the bottom drawer of the file cabinet. The phone is ringing.

He nods to the phone. "No funny business," he says.

I wonder what funny business I could possibly try. On the phone is a voice both excited and controlled, going on like the Ferguson after Ben fitted it with a governor.

"Hello, is this Matty Keillor? You probably don't know me, but then again you might. I've seen you at some weddings. I work for the *Post Crescent* now and I understand Cecil Alt's in there with you. I heard about it on the radio. And it just about drove me crazy, you know, because once, just after high school, I dated Cecil. I mean, I actually went to the movies with him once. Really. And I said that and my editor heard me and so now I wonder if I could talk with him. Cecil, I mean. Usually I write the fashion articles, but this is really a break for me, you know what I mean?"

"It's for you," I say to Cecil. "You want to talk?"

"Who is it?"

"I don't know," I lie. It would take too long to explain it to him.

"Bring me the phone. Slow. No funny stuff."

Cecil talks like he's seen one too many Dragnet shows, but learned only the henchman parts. He used to laugh and make jokes. He was the flip side of Frankie. Now he's slipped beyond even where Frankie is.

The woman on the phone is Crystal Donleavy. Cystal must be twenty-five now. She talked to Rose at the last wedding we attended, Bill Meyers and Connie Jacobsen. Crystal was dressed like a secretary who reads ladies' magazines. At one time she could have been a model in a small way. Her hair is Scandinavian white gold, her lips full, her skin fine porcelain, her build thin and lanky, her eyes doe-like. It was her high rounded forehead that kept her out of modelling, that and a habit of letting her shoulders round off, rather than pulling them back square. And she walked like a camel. Her body arrived a stride off-pace with where her feet touched earth. Once she was in a local VFW Women's Auxiliary fashion show and she clomped down the runway as if the oasis were just ahead.

She's done all right for herself, though. I've seen her by-line a few times in the Women's section of the paper, and she told Rose she was engaged to a lawyer in Fon du Lac and her life was finally becoming attendant to perfection. That was her phrase: attendant to perfection. Crystal is the kind of proud camel-footed woman who would unconsciously use such a phrase to such a person as Rose. Rose, whose body is more gnarled every year with congenital arthritis, and who has not been far from a pair of crutches since she was eight. Rose, who was never asked to any dance, never had any beau and never will, whose male friends see in her sexless but cheery companionship, a surface view of her that fails to recognize her longing, her desire to be hugged: they imagine her a beech tree, twisted by wind and age and its own imperceptible yearnings to bulge and knot and curl into itself. They think, stupidly, that she is comfortable with the wreckage of her own body only because at twenty-five she's still as spirited as she was at seven.

Rose has a thatch of straight brown hair cut like a boy's (like mine) and freckles are strewn across her face, some blotched together, and one front tooth's broken in half from when she last tried to mount a bicycle. And to this person Crystal Donleavy, beautiful, tall, straight except through her own sloth, living in a modern apartment in downtown Appleton, lights a cigarette and says her life is becoming, "attendant to perfection."

I don't think Cecil Alt has worked on an Edsel in over three years. He stopped when his father first took sick. Yet now he's talking to Crystal about carburetors. I can't imagine that conversation going anywhere on the strength of a failed evening seven years ago, but it continues. Crystal's got more talent, after all, than I thought.

Cecil puts the phone down but he doesn't hang up.

"She said to leave the phone off the hook. I can talk to her whenever I like."

"What if someone else wants to talk with you?" I'm thinking of the police, or a psychologist, or anybody. I see myself in a tree with Cecil, and a fireman climbing up a long aluminum ladder to reach us.

Cecil is firm. "Nobody wants to talk with me," he says. "Only Crystal."

Cecil and Frankie weren't ever really friends, but they slept in the same room for years. Ben and Cecil, Sr. exchanged sons for working purposes frequently. In summer Cecil ate at our table two or three times a week. Yet I'd never say I knew him. His was another mouth full of my pot roast. Alice must've thought the same thing about Frankie. And I think, too, we both must think the same thing about our own children. Did I ever know Frankie? Did she know Cecil?

Frankie and Cecil didn't even know each other. Cecil worked hard and was shy. At the dinner table I watched his eyes bulge when Frankie grabbed the last hunk of bread from under Ben's reaching fingers and calmly said, "Beat you, old man," and then buttered the bread and ate it, washing it down with a long gulp of milk. Frankie moved too fast for Ben and Cecil, too fast for everybody.

Frankie was probably the first or second person in Augsbury to try drugs other than alcohol, and he was despised for that. I could tell when he was doing something: besides the eyes and his tendency to sweat, he spoke from a place I couldn't recognize. The words coming from his mouth were coming from a long way away. They weren't part of the world familiar to me. Frankie could speak in tongues, only the floor thrashing he did was not in any way religious. I saw him once by the hay mow, he was to be feeding the hogs and hadn't yet and it was getting on towards dusk. There he was, on the edge of the open barn floor, rolling in the loose straw, broken stalks tacked to his shirt, dust rising, his face grey, saliva dripping on his chin, his eyes wild. I fed the hogs myself and hauled him to his room. I locked him in. I told Ben Frankie'd gone out drinking. When Frankie came down the next morning Ben beat him for drinking, but I shudder to think of the beating he'd have gotten if Ben'd found him as I had, a sprawled animal, barking because of the demons inside.

When the letter came in 1966, Frankie packed a duffle bag and announced that for the good of himself, and the good of the world, particularly that green spot on the map once called French Indochina (and still called that on the map in our encyclopedia, though there it's colored purple), he was going to Canada.

A long time passed. I expected a letter from Canada (Ben had written him off as no longer being a son as soon as the screen door slammed, Ben's curses and screams of "Coward!" still full in the air), but when the letter came it was postmarked New Mexico. Fits and starts after that. A batch of postcards, all New Mexico, all short, his handwriting filling the back of the card with a sentence and a half—"Have work in a filling station. Not much, but—". Or, "89° today. Cement boils down here. My feet hurt and it's only one o'clock."

Then nothing for a long time. Finally, he wrote from Palo Alto, California. It was the spring of 1968. Rupert had gone over and come back. Frankie was living with a woman and farming. Working as a hired hand for a truck farmer, really. Then a postcard from San Francisco. The woman was pregnant and he was running away. He never said that, but it's something I know. Ben didn't want to know anything. A letter would come and he didn't want to hear it. "Frankie's in Australia," I'd say one lunch. "You want to hear about it? He's eating dog meat and says it's better than you'd think." Ben would shake his head. "Don't pay to find out what the dead are up to," he said.

Four and a half years after he first left he came back. Ben tried to have no part of him. "Sleep in the barn," he said. It was December. "Sleep with the hogs. Eat their swill. You been doing it everyplace else."

Then he cried. Cried and took Frankie, who was at first indifferent but then cried, too, into his arms. "God damn you, Frankie," Ben said. They drank whiskey in short glasses in front of the fire. Steam rose from their socks.

I look to where Cecil's finishing off another long sip. His feet jump on the floor nervously, the gun in his lap bounces as if it were a child he was trying to put to sleep. It's been some time since anybody called inside. I wonder if Jones has gotten up the gumption to admit this isn't something he can handle. Has he called the Appleton police yet? Or is he on the verge of something foolish and stupid? It's not just crises that Jones bungles, he's taken for a dim bulb on everyday things, too. Three years back about this time of year Jones tried cracking down on speeders by waiting for them by the A & W stand, eyes glued to his brand-new radar gun, and lighted out after them as they flashed by. Then somebody—some say Dana and Norbert Krake—snuck up behind him, pressed ether into his face, one of them holding him, and when he woke up he was trussed and strung between two posts supporting the drive-in roof. Today, he's parked his car in Cecil Alt's line of fire.

I've learned not to expect much from Clayton Jones.

What I expect instead is for this whole thing to peter out. Cecil'll run out of shells and that'll be that.

That's not really what I expect. What I expect I dare not voice. It would escape from me and somehow become tangible. It would take on substance and happen. Shots would be fired, people would be dead. This day would become a chronicle of needless tragedy, a T.V. docu-drama, a movie of the week that people in New York and Los Angeles would take as an emblem of the disease (their word for it would be "malaise") that's affecting America even at her heart.

It's nothing of the kind.

It's just something that's happened and will stop happening when the reasons for it lose their hold on poor, twisted Cecil Alt.

At least I am no longer subject to the hysterical ravings and mindless chatter of Leona Griemerts.

I wonder what she's saying to them, outside? Has her brief terror become fit stuff for a special report on Channel Five's Noon Show? Are the radio stations beaming her scared voice into other homes? Is her voice even now changing from that of victim to celebrity? Are the soap operas being interrupted? Am I being equated to Leona Griemerts? Is she my spokesman?

Such questions are below me. I'm jealous because she has the opportunity to be the fool and I don't.

Cecil stands up. "Outgoing!" he shouts. He fires both barrels. Slugs ram into the cars across the street. The cars grunt in response.

Jones shouts, "Jesus Christ, Cecil, lay off, would you?"

"I can keep this up all day," Cecil says, reloading.

"But why?" Jones asks. It's the same voice of personal hurt he used when begging someone to cut him down three years ago.

"I got nothing to say to you," Cecil says.

I hear Jones say to someone, "Tell the Donleavy girl to call the town hall again."

I had hung up the phone while Cecil wasn't looking. I'd hoped someone, someone with some sense, would call Cecil and talk him into giving himself up. But maybe Crystal'll be better for Cecil than somebody who does know what he's doing but doesn't know Cecil.

That time Frankie came back he didn't stay long. He explained he needed to be elsewhere (his child, I thought) and had stopped here only long enough to say hello. Besides, he said, it was dangerous to be here very long—someone might see him and report him.

"Who'd do something like that?" I said.

Frankie looked at Ben and said, "Jones."

"You're not saying everything, boy," Ben said. "You come here for other reasons than a visit, didn't you?"

Frankie looked at his feet.

"We don't have shit, your Ma and me," Ben said. "And we've got no reason to give you money. You run off like a damned fool and you stayed foolish while you been gone." Ben went to his desk and wrote a check. "Good money after bad is what this is." He snapped the book shut and put it away. "Come back the next time when you don't have this kind of reason."

Frankie hasn't been back. It's been nearly twelve years. Ben died and Frankie didn't come. Rupert died, and Frankie didn't come. When he writes he includes no address. The postmark is Houston. He has a woman and child. I'd feel better if I could see them, but I won't, not in this life.

"I need coffee," Cecil tells me.

"It's in the next room—the police office."

"Go get some. But any funny business . . . ." He pats his gun just ahead of the hammer.

I nod. I pick up Leona's mug—mine was blown to smithereens along with the desk—and head down the hall. I'm seven feet from the outside. If I were a younger woman, I'd take my chances and dive through the front door, risking the broken glass and twisted metal, praying to God Cecil wouldn't actually shoot with calm precision the woman who fed him corn on the cob, lima beans, and pot roast some fifteen years ago.

Instead I go into the office. At the doorway I see the barricade, I see Jones on a walkie talkie. His round pink face struggles with composure. It looks as if his eyes are about to pop from their sockets and the rest of his face break into tiny pieces from some internal pressure. He doesn't see me. I slip into the police office and after I get the water running, I sit down.

Lord, my hands are shaking. Nothing is clear. I could climb on top of Jones' desk, pull open the louvered window above and get their attention out in the street. They'd know I'm safe and Cecil alone. In that way they could go for him. He couldn't come for me without coming down the hall. I wouldn't get out till they had gotten him, though. I'd have to hear it: shouts, shots. Cecil?

No.

But I could, when I get their attention, ask them to pull me out. The window is small, but I'd fit through. It'd take some time, but Jones or someone must be capable of pulling an old woman through a window.

That still leaves Cecil. He might come out quietly, but I don't know. What's prompted him today will not submit to quiet resolution.

I think about my other choice while I rinse out Leona's cup and rinse a new one for myself. I can stay right here. Not motion for help. Just be here, safe. Wait. Jailed, perhaps, but safe. Between the outside and Cecil's inside.

What will that get me? I'll sit here as I am now, my hands still quivering as with palsy, like Ben's. I won't be anywhere. A child frozen in the birthing channel. To be between things is to be nowhere at all.

Where is Rupert? I buried him in November—Ben was the last day of October—and I can go to Morningside and point to his stone (under an alder tree, with a patch of sycamores just to the left and beyond) and say, "There is Rupert," but that says nothing. To give the catechism answer, to say he's in heaven, is to say even less.

As for where he was: You'd never have thought a Mama's boy, as Frankie and Matthew and Ben called him, would end up at a sawmill in Stevenson, Missouri, but he did. Perhaps he was there to prove first to himself alone that he was not what he'd been called. After the service he stayed here until the last two years, doing odd jobs, never heavy work, and then he said he was going out on his own. "But not like Frankie," he said. "I'm going to make something of myself."

Rupert wrote of the peace he'd found. Yes, there was the buzzsaw racket and the sawdust flying, but in the midst of the din he could hear himself, thinking clearly. He had a future and he could see it—learn the sawmill trade there in Missouri, learn it thoroughly, properly, and then return to Augsbury. He could buy into Lanstry's Lumber easy, old Lanstry was not a good lumberman and ran a poor business which he hadn't gotten out of yet because no one'd offered to take it off his hands. Being just down from the Kafka Feed and Seed was a prime location, and with proper managing Lanstry's would turn a profit.

Rupert had other ideas that came to him, too, whether through the mill noise or at his trailer home I don't know. He wanted to get married, but not until he'd turned Lanstry's around. I laughed when he wrote he didn't know exactly who he'd marry, but once Lanstry's was Rupert Keillor's he didn't expect that to be a problem. "And we're going to have children," he wrote. "Three fat pink ones."

The light on Jones' phone is flashing. It's the town hall extension—Crystal must be talking to Cecil again. What can she say to him? What can she possibly say? I imagine Cecil pouring his heart out to her in the mistaken belief he's filling her loving cup rather than her newspad, but I cannot think what Crystal would say back to him. Cecil is not someone who's worth her while to impress. But then, neither was Rose.

I climb on top of Bud's desk, the one facing the back wall. On tip toes I can see out to the river. In summer it's sluggish, creeping between the rocks and beer cans and old shells that litter its bed. Hunters often go there for squirrel and grouse in the ravine, though it's illegal inside town limits. Not that it matters since Jones is often out there himself.

But in the spring, now, the river dances. Children fish for bluegills and sunfish at Black Otter Lake's spillway, which feeds the river, gives it life. I pull down the window and I can hear the gurgling, the play of water over rock. Above the creek a grey squirrel leaps from bare tree to bare tree, his tight body stark against the sky. He's scavenging for what he's already picked clean this winter.

If I've thought little of my other children there's a reason: they've not led lives which weigh heavily on me.

Isabel lives in Bloomington, Minnesota. She finished school there two years ago and works with the hearing impaired. She and Frankie are the two brunettes in a family of blondes. Her current beau is not someone I expect she'll marry—she's very particular in such matters—but he was kind enough when I saw them last. Tony, I think his name is, a shiny-haired intern at St. Catherine's. Isabel's current tastes run towards professional men and I suspect when one really catches her fancy she'll marry him, not just live with him. What I've seen with Amanda I don't foresee with Isabel. Isabel may be occasionally cold-blooded in her doings, but when she settles into something it's heart and soul.

Amanda's the reverse. She married Leotis Brown heart and soul two years out of high school and now she's cold-blooded about everything. Between Leotis and herself, that's one thing. The distance between them is common enough to people everywhere and it's a distance I've no business trying to close. Their rift is their business, though I have to say Leotis did little to find himself on the side he's on. A solider man you cannot find. He works hard and looks at people square. He's not overly affectionate, but I've known few men who are who've not caught heat for letting the soft part of themselves show.

It's with no small pride I remember when Amanda was Homecoming Queen, her hair piled high on her head, a wide pink belt tight under her bodice, the blue and silver banner crossing over that. After high school she spent two years in the paper mill. She got a belly. Her cheeks got full, her eyes puffy. Leotis paid her attention and she spruced up again. Stopped guzzling beer like a millhand, wore dresses at night. She was beautiful again at her wedding.

What has gone on since then between her and Leotis should not touch her children. Their flesh is hers and she must hold to that.

She doesn't. I've seen her eat steak and feed them hot dogs. She buys herself a new array of Avon cosmetics while Tommy and Scott have toes poking through holey socks and holey shoes. She wears nice sweaters and her children sniffle. The children squabble as children do, and she slaps without consideration. Her justice miscarries. It's all heat and thunder. Her children fear her. They call me Mamoosh and leap to me when I come over. They can tell that though my affection is thin, it's evenly distributed. To Amanda, Dorie has possibilities and the boys are dirt. She sees in Dorie the glimmer of a future homecoming queen and she is shaping the child to that end. Already Dorie's blue eyes and smile shine and don't as if by a switch. She's only twelve; I fear for what she'll become.

Fred I've never had fears about. As a baby his heart was strong, good (he kicked harder than any of them), and he's grown up the same—plump in the face and hardy.

He's marrying a Hanratty come September. She's twenty-two, Fred's just barely twenty-three, but there are few people I know who are better suited for the business of marriage. After her mother died, Mary Hanratty looked after her two sisters and her brother from when she was thirteen on. That girl knows stout mothering. Her head's on her shoulders, her feet on the ground. It's with the coasters, the ones who fall in love with toes barely touching soil, that things turn sour.

That's not true either. Ben went sour and if ever there was a man with his feet planted, it was Ben. But with Ben it was the physical thing that eventually turned his mind. He'd have stayed good if his body hadn't failed him.

I'm making excuses. I made no excuses for Rose, whose body betrayed her much sooner than Ben's, and Rose has stayed true. Early on I expected to make allowances for Rose and I've found I haven't needed to. Rose is whole in her heart and that's not something I can say about most of my children. Isabel, perhaps. Fred, yes. The others—Matthew got out too soon. He left when he was twenty-seven and yet he left too soon for me to know his heart. First born, first out, but I thought he'd just always be here. Amanda's heart is sour, sour as ditch water, and Frankie's heart is strong, but filled with confusions and they've spun him around.

And Rupert? Rupert's heart was getting stronger even as he collapsed inside, unlike Ben, whose heart, body, mind, everything, collapsed in stages without order, like an abandoned house goes. The middle sagging first, then the porch, the stairs, lintels, roof—falling at random, but surely falling. I'll say this for Ben, though. When Cecil, Sr. died, Ben put aside his bottles and became clearheaded. Ben, for that last week, tried it Cecil's way—without the drunken inwardness that had become his philosophy. "A body can't die like this," he said one night, stone drunk, his hand shaking off the bannister as I helped him up the stairs. "Look at this," he said, pulling up his sleeve to show the purple-scarred burn line where they'd tried mustard gas a few months before. For three days that final week he shook worse than ever, the alcohol going out of him, leaving behind only shivers. More hollow than ever, but clean. For three more days he was bright, or nearly so. He joked. "Plant me upside down. My thoughts're always better when my feet are elevated."

Then he died.

Those last seven days he had heart enough for all of us. Myself, I don't know about anymore. My heart's faint sometimes when it just shouldn't be. I've kept quiet with Cecil for several hours now because I lack the courage to speak. The words falter even as I conceive them. I'd try to wrench them from my tongue, say something when I bring him coffee, but what can I say to a man who could splinter me with one anxious finger? I wasn't always like this. Once on a Saturday in September Bernice Brudecki called me, hysterical, crying and shouting into the phone to come over quick, Neil'd gotten his hand caught in the corn picker trying to unjam it and it'd taken four of his fingers off.

I drove over in the Impala, marvelling at Neil's stupidity in trying to unjam a moving piece of machinery. When I got there, though, I had no time for marvelling at anybody's stupidity. Bernice was throwing up in the bathroom and Neil sat in the kitchen with his face pale as over-blanched peas, his hand wrapped in sheets and tucked tight under his arm. The sheets were violent red.

"We've got to find those fingers," I said. "I'll be right back. Meantime, call an ambulance."

Bernice nodded weakly.

I ran out to the field where the tractor was still idling. I shut everything off and opened the gear box on the side of the picker. Pieces of corn stalk and blood splattered everywhere. Someplace in the grease and the gore were Neil's fingers. I found one. A white bit of bone gleamed from where the knuckle fit onto the hand. I guessed it was his index finger. It was fairly mangled. I made a pouch with the front of my dress and carried it back to the house. Neil was flapping his arm down on his hand trying to get more pressure on it.

"I only found one," I said. "How soon before the ambulance?"

"Bernice is still in the bathroom," he said. "She won't come out."

I yelled, "This is your husband, you chicken shit," but the bathroom door was closed. Bernice didn't answer.

"You should be on your way to the hospital," I said. "I'll drive you."

At the hospital they sewed Neil's hand to his stomach so skin would grow back on the stumps. The finger turned out to be his ring finger, though his wedding band was never found. What I'd recovered was useless. His index finger is now a potato-like lump—part of it had been left on the hand when the auger took the rest of it.

A worse accident happened four years ago when I was with Rupert getting groceries. We were the second car that stopped at a collision. A car had gone off the pavement (clear day, dry pavement) and smashed into a power pole. The driver, the only one in the car, was thrown halfway through the windshield. His gut was impaled on the glass supporting him. I've done two hundred and fifty chickens in an afternoon, wrung their necks and bled them one after another and there was never blood like this. The first person had a CB and he'd already called for help. Police and the ambulance came at the same time. Rupert stayed in the car, white-faced. He couldn't even get his door open. The man with the CB got inside his own car and vomited on the floor between his legs. He'd picked up a piece of turf that rested against the hood ornament—the car was an old Chrysler—and the turf turned out to be the dying man's scalp.

I helped the medics and a policeman get the man off the windshield. What looked like empty sausage casings dangled wetly from the sharp edges of glass where the man's stomach had been. He moaned and blood came out of his mouth.

None of it affected me until Rupert and I were a quarter mile down the road. Rupert's face was still white, like moist chalk, and all of a sudden I felt the heat go out of my own face. My fingers felt frozen on the wheel and my throat got tight and sand dry. I tried to swallow and I couldn't. I had to pull off the road and roll down the window, let cool air gust in so I could breathe, so I could swallow.

Since then I'm queasy at the sight of blood. Just thinking about it sets me off. I have to force myself to look when somebody's hurt. To not look but think about it is worse than looking and dealing with it. I'm sick just the same.

The light on Jones' phone is still lit, which means Crystal and Cecil are still at it. I'll wait till they're finished before I go back.

What if I listened? What Crystal and Cecil say to each other is no business of mine, except in a roundabout way. But what if Cecil turns ugly because of what Crystal says or doesn't say to him?

With great care I lift the receiver and cover the mouthpiece with my hand. Cecil is crying. Crystal is assuring him, "Of course, I'll go out with you again, Cecil." From her urgency I'd guess this has been going on for some time. Cecil's sobs lack depth, they come out of him in short breaths. His whole body must be shaking.

Crystal says, "Cecil, I'd love to see you again. I only said no before because I had things going on those nights. And then you stopped calling, and you know a woman doesn't call a man for a date."

Cecil gulps air for an answer, as if he's been under water for a long time.

"Cecil, my editor wants to know why you thought it was a good idea to take over the town hall?"

I hang up then. Even if Cecil were able enough to give an answer, I doubt that whatever he said could be even close to what was true.

I climb on Jones' desk. His faces Roosevelt Avenue. Byron Joe is sucking down a Pabst on the bridge. His right hand rests on the trunk of Bud's car, as if daring Cecil to shoot again. I can see no reason why Byron Joe is on the bridge other than he's Byron Joe and who's going to tell him to move? He takes a pause in guzzling and looks up and down the street, his face flat with scorn. Then he sees me. His is a scowl that makes you question what it is you're doing being alive and so weak, so insignificant. He snorts to himself and finishes his can. With one hand he crushes the can and boots it towards the front door of the town hall. He salutes me with two fingers and cracks his knuckles. Just beyond the barriers are about a half dozen police cars, mostly county cops, plus two state patrol cars and a police van. Most of the people have been shooed away. Herb Tessen is still there, though. It must be a chill wind that's reddened his knuckles and face. His hair is flopped back, showing how pinkly bald he really is. He combs long strands of black and grey hair from one ear across to the other so it looks like he's not, but he plasters his hair with enough grease to make you think of nothing else. He looks like he's being knifed from behind. He's standing there, no doubt, as a testament to love. He probably cajoled Jones to let him. "Just stay out of the way," Jones probably said, as if Herb would do something dramatic to save me. No, Herb will wait in the wings till this is over. Then, heart pounding relief, he'll console me upon my deliverence, or, given the worst, set up a public wailing.

Then again, maybe I just want someone to feel that way.

Byron Joe has strolled over to Herb. A man in a dark suit and a tan overcoat is there talking with Jones and five or six uniformed policemen. Byron Joe taps the suited man on the shoulder and grins. His other hand comes down heavy on Herb's shoulder. Byron Joe rarely finds things this funny.

I have no explanation for the fury welling inside me. Quickly I fill the two coffee mugs and scamper back down the hall.

Jones' voice is behind me. "Matty, what in hell are you doing?" But I've already ducked into my office. Cecil gets up from the phone and sights down the hallway. He sends two more shells thumping into the cars across the street.

Jones' voice is a whine. "Damn it, Matty, another minute and you'd've been out."

He's right. I lean past Cecil. "You're not killing him."

"We've no intention, ma'am. If Cecil'll just put the gun down everything will be all right."

I'm guessing that's the overcoat man.

I look at Cecil. He gives me a cocked-head quizzical look like a dog about to scratch himself. Then he shakes his head.

"Cecil says no go."

"Is that him saying or you saying?" Jones asks.

"What do you think?"

"Any fool would've walked when the chance was there."

The overcoat man has a point. What pushed me back—my fear for Cecil? Or for myself? This can't go on. I used to feed him. He used to stand by the fenceline at dusk with a beer in his hand, watching the horses run. Even then he was six foot something or other and drawn out like a hoe handle. Sitting down at my kitchen table he could look me in the eye. Now I'm determined to look him in the eye. First I must summon my voice. I've used it for him, but not yet to him. I look at my hands, each still holding a mug of coffee.

"I hope you like it black," I say. "I think you used to take it with cream, but I didn't have time."

"I understand," he says. "Black's fine."

We stare at each other. Cecil tries to smile, the lips folding in on themselves unevenly, without parting. "You did a good thing," he says and goes back to the phone, coffee in hand. He settles into his chair and says to Crystal, "Matty's back and they're mad at her."

I'm mad at myself. Cecil is not my child and yet I've done something I would only do for one of my own. And I haven't always done that for my own. When Rupert caught sick in a way nobody knew, not the company doctor, not the Stevenson City Hospital doctors, not even the people at the Mayo Clinic, it was not me who went to him. It was Fred and Isabel.

Twice I took the Greyhound to Rochester (I didn't trust myself on a long drive, my head distracted by grief). The first time I stayed a week. The second time only a weekend. I told myself this short-changing of my son was because I was needed at home—Rose needed someone—but Rose has managed for herself better than I allow and she'll continue to when I'm no longer able. She'll probably attend to us both soon enough. No, it wasn't Rose who held me in Augsbury during the two and a half months of Rupert's sickness, and it wasn't Ben either. Ben would have understood my shuttling from one deathbed to another. And it was a full month after Ben was gone that I could've seen Rupert and I didn't go once. And that one weekend I did go hardly counts, seeing him briefly in two days, the second time briefer than the first. It was a failure of heart.

Isabel and Fred made no such excuses. Isabel was close and visited every weekend, sometimes on weeknights. And Fred—Fred postponed his wedding a full year. He and Mary wanted a September wedding. He also wanted Ben to see him married, but when Rupert dropped with some sort of lung mold no one could diagnose except for guessing that it might have something to do with Rupert's breathing in moist particles of sawdust and correctly identifying its most terrifying symptom, that of Rupert coughing up blood and eventually pieces of his lungs, Fred explained to Mary that Rupert needed him. Fred took what money he was saving to get married with and rented a room in Rochester. And he did what I could not, what I shied from doing: he sat with Rupert and read him the *Press-Star* when it came on Fridays and read him books, books that Fred would never have read but that Rupert liked, "real literature shit," Fred said later. And Fred turned the channels on the T.V. set, and they followed the fall baseball games and the early part of the Packer season and Fred wiped blood off Rupert's chin and hands when he coughed it up and helped him to the bathroom and helped him back and sat there while Rupert pushed his food around his plate, because as the weeks wore on Rupert lost all interest in eating, and Fred joked with him, saying that for an older brother he sure was getting babied, and Fred held him at night when the dark and lack of sound and the stench of his own decaying body, the sour smell of himself rotting inside that hung at the back of his throat, was all too much for Rupert and he gave in to tears and sobbing, the sobbing bringing fits of coughing, phlegm and blood being hacked out onto his hands and getting smeared on the sheets, with Jesus-God and his mother nowhere close to comforting him.

The last time I saw Rupert was the last weekend in October. Halloween was a few days off, so was the Feast of All Souls. Fred and Isabel had decorated Rupert's room with black and orange crepe paper—streamers arcing from the light fixtures to the walls and hanging from the walls to the floor. A carved pumpkin grinned on his bedside table, a lit candle inside scorching its skull cap. Amanda and Matthew had sent greeting cards. Rose's card, with a letter, was in my purse. Even Frankie sent a postcard from Houston—how he found out about Rupert I don't know, though I guess he and Fred were sometimes in contact—a plain white one, with "Hang in there, bro" written on the back. I had brought candy and a blue cotton shirt. Fred helped him sit up so he could try the shirt on.

"I would've liked a costume, Mom. It's nearly Halloween."

"You're too old for that kind of thing," I said.

"A sheet with two eye holes, maybe. I need the practice. Or maybe diapers.

I'm shitting yellow anyway."

"Don't give up, Rupert." Isabel stroked his forehead. She pushed his hair away from his eyes. "The doctors here are the best in the world. You couldn't be at a better place."

"Hold my hand, Mom."

Rupert looked so small. As if I were seeing him from a great distance. As if I were seeing him as a tiny child again. He was holding out his hand.

"I'm all jelly inside, Ma. Please, hold my hand."

"It's okay," Fred said. He took Rupert's hand in both of his. Rupert didn't seem to be focusing on anything, but his eyes illuminated me like headlights. I caught their shine and I couldn't move. He knew I wasn't coming back.

"Hold me, Mama, hold me."

There is a shame in my heart I can never remove. On All Soul's Day I prayed that God grant mercy on the souls entrusted to Him. I prayed for Ben, whom I buried the previous day; I prayed for Rupert, whom God would claim before the month was out; I prayed for Rose and Fred and Isabel and Frankie and Amanda and Matthew, whom I was losing or had lost. I did not have the courage to pray for myself.

Cecil Alt has done me no crime that I haven't done to myself. Both before and after my last trip to Rochester and at the same time Ben was, finally, cleansing himself of the alcohol he'd used to dull the pain that kept reminding him he was still alive, I became a wanton horror unto myself. Something inside me gave way, perhaps a further collapse of heart that allowed the foulness in me to run free. I called Porter Atwood.

I called Porter Atwood, who'd been around several times that summer and again in the fall, and told him I was thinking of selling some acreage.

I let Porter wine and dine me the day before I went to see Rupert. I let him get me tipsy. I laughed at his jokes. I let him put his hand over mine at the dinner table at the Red Ox. I let him toast me. Porter, with a wife at home and two kids in school. And later, in a room at the Paper Valley Inn in Appleton I let him do things no man but Ben has ever done. And the night before Ben died I went to him again. Called him and then met him at the hotel. I was doing these things mechanically. I don't recall anything about those nights.

That's a lie. What I remember is his fingertips parting my blouse, his coming inside me (too soon, too soon), his patting my rump later, as if I were a dog. I thrilled at his touch and I despised him for believing that when he was done, I was done. I remember him looking in the mirror, too, afterwards, and I remember thinking any man that conceited probably always got what he wanted.

From me he got eighty acres.

With Ben's death I came to my senses. Slowly, as if they'd all been dulled and I didn't know the proper way to use any of them. My fingers strayed onto my cheeks as if they'd never been there before. The smell of coffee and the phone ringing were somehow connected and I'd get them confused.

With Rupert's death I achieved clarity. It was suddenly obvious a second mortgage from the bank would have done, with no loss of dignity, what two evenings with Porter Atwood had done. When I think of how afterwards he made sure his string tie with the scorpion slide hung just so down his shirt and then pecked me on the cheek, my lips quiver, I have palpitations. To whom do I explain?

I clear my throat. "Cecil," I say, "Cecil, I've done some horrible things."

Cecil looks up from his feet. "I'm telling Crystal that very thing. I'm telling her the bad I've done in my life. But I'm not like you, Matty. I can't give reasons for what I've done." Cecil's eyes return to his feet, and my whole body—feet, face, extremities—tingles as if, some seconds ago, my hands closed round a strand of electrified fence.

Cecil has put the phone down. He has another pull at the bottle and he sucks the whiskey back over his teeth with the sound of a cat hissing. He lets out a yawn. He yawns again and closes his eyes. His one hand twitches and slips from the gun on his lap. His head has fallen forward and then the room is filled with his gentle snore. It is like perfume, reaching every corner.

I go to Cecil and comb his hair with my fingers. His head nods dreamily. From outside Jones' voice booms in, louder than it needs to be. "You got ten minutes, Cecil. You hear me? Ten minutes. We got tear gas now. We're not fooling around, Cecil. Not foolin' around anymore at all."

My fingers continue to go through Cecil's thin hair. When the children were young I did that with each of them. The last thing I did before pulling the covers over their small bodies and closed the door was comb their hair in place. The girls in one room, the boys in another. Then I'd go downstairs and collapse in the easy chair, the one with the quilted cover. One night Ben was in the kitchen doing figures.

"Are we broke yet?" I asked.

"I'm working on it," he said. "But there's just enough here that I can't say we're flat out busted."

"Come here," I said. And he pushed back his cap, the De Kalb with the feed dust dirtying the wings, and came to me, a grin across his brown face. He sat in my lap and I combed his hair with my fingers. His hair was thinning even then, but each strand was fat and wiry, the color of rust. His thumb and forefinger played with my earlobe.

"What do you think?" he said. "I mean, what's gonna happen?"

It wasn't a question Ben had ever asked me before. Ben had ideas about how the world was run and even when his experience ran counter to his ideas he didn't alter them. "We'll see," he'd say and wait for the long haul of time to bear him out. Since his own ideas were fixed, he had little need for mine. So when he asked me, "What's gonna happen?", I wasn't sure if I felt great joy or sadness.

"I don't know," I said. "Why do you ask?"

"No reason," he said.

If I were to know, would I have told him? Could I have believed it myself? Could I have continued to believe in anything at all, as, somehow, I do? Could there really be a God this vengeful and petty, this needlessly spiteful, this cruel?

I say that without conviction. All my children are living but one and Cecil Alt is asleep in his chair. My husband's death was a blessing to all, a blow to nothing but my fondness for life, however crippled.

It's better to accept grief than turn it away. I was told that by my mother before my own wedding. And when I taught catechism after school to the Catholic children who went to the public school (some of them were mine) I told them the same thing. I told them that grief and joy come to you unbidden, without you asking, and you had to do your best to accept what you were given, because all things come from God. And by accepting what comes from God you are partaking of the eternal.

I told them that, yet I miss combing Ben's hair.

And standing here now, my fingers deep in Cecil's thin hair, I think of how the eternal must be bound up in such moments, such gestures. They'll find us like this—Cecil asleep and my back to the door, bent over the dreaming Cecil as if he were my own.

STEPHERS

The summer I found out about my mother I took up diving, having spent the last three summers learning to swim. My mother or Mrs. Talperi would drive me and my brother Jeremy and the Nelson twins and Tina Talperi to the Lake Park Pool where we progressed from Beginners to Intermediate to Advanced. Only by the end of that first summer I was in Advanced and Jeremy stayed in Beginners through the second summer, which is when I took water safety and canoeing. I hated canoeing. The paddle was an awkward stick, too big at one end, and I was too fascinated by the spangles in the water and by the gurgling whirlpools left by my stroke to notice whether I was in stroke or not. My partner was older and resented being teamed with a girl and resented it even more when I was in back and supposed to be steering and he'd turn to me, the whole canoe walla-walling, and shout at me to pay attention. The third summer I began leaping off the low board at a full gallop and managed, by mid-August, to lean over from the high board and then fall off, head-first and more or less gracefully, into the cool silty green water below, a plummeting I previously only could stomach feet first and with my eyes closed, my toes scrunched and one small fist clamped over my nostrils, my other arm clenched across my waist, my whole body rigid with the fear that any appendage not closed down tight against myself would be torn off by the merciless water.

It turned out not to be so. What was so was, terror notwithstanding, I was quite good at plummeting some five meters into three of water with no splash—just a thlupp! and widening ripples. The swim instructor, a Mr. Gordon (Gordon Gordon, it turned out—why would parents do such a thing? I wondered. It sounded like a name Jeremy would come up with for one of his ever-expiring turtles), talked to my parents in September and asked if he couldn't work with me on just diving all the next summer. He was the high school swimming coach and wanted me on his team the following year. After his phone call my parents explained all this to me and said it would be my decision. "He says you're remarkable," my mother said. I said I wasn't sure. "She's got all winter," my father said. "Let her decide in the spring." I realized they'd decided for me as if I weren't in the room.

"You'll go to the Olympicth," Jeremy said. He said it as if he were going. "You'll be famouth!"

I looked at Jeremy with my "I'd-tolerate-you-if-you-weren't-so-dumb" look. He punched me high in the arm with one knuckle extended and shouted, "Olympicth! Olympicth!" dancing on the carpet and waving his hands.

"Jeremy, shut up," my father said and Jeremy sat back down.

Nobody said anything about his hitting me. It was as if it were allowed.

There was a man next door to us at the time. He'd moved in in September and he was doing what my mother was, too, only I don't think my mother was yet. Our house was built on a slowly rising hill and his house sat below ours by several feet so our front porch looked into his first floor bedroom. All fall and winter there were different women. The women would always be on top of him, shoulders thrown back, their breasts erect or not depending on their size. I would stand by the side window in our entranceway in the time between my father's departure for work and my mother's and I would watch them. Sometimes he took them to his upstairs bedroom which I could see into from my bedroom. Later I would check my own breasts against those I saw. I tried to imagine myself, what it would be like, with the fullness and the weight. The darker nipples. In my room I touched my own, my fingertips teasing them erect and I wondered what it was like to have someone else, a man, touch them in that way.

Tina Talperi thought I was nuts. "Men don't do that!" she said. "They just grab and hold on."

"How do you know?" I said.

"I've seen my parents," she said solemnly.

In the spring afternoons the man next door would be on his front porch playing with his dog. He'd be dressed in white painter's pants or blue jeans and his shirts were striped. Even sitting down his knees poked the air in front of him as he read the paper and absentmindedly tossed the stick his dog kep retrieving. He was home earlier than anyone else in the neighborhood—three-thirty or four every day he'd be with his paper and his black dog with the plumed tail curling over its back like a watch spring.

My mother was prodding me to study diving with Gordon Gordon. "I've already signed Jeremy up for Intermediate," she said. "You'll have to take something because we don't have the money for camp."

What camp? I wanted to know. No one around us sent their children to camp. It was a stupid idea and I thought maybe it had something to do with the martinis. My parents had started drinking martinis before dinner, an idea gotten from who knows where, and even though they commented on how awful they tasted, they kept trying them.

The man next door had a tall glass of tomato juice-and-something next to him while he read. A squat piece of yellowy green celery stuck out the top like a flag. He looked like he could sit there on those porch steps with his tomato juice-and-something and his paper and his dog and be that way forever. All winter I'd just seen the white length of himself with one woman or another perched on him where his hips and waist met. His stomach rose like a horse's rump and the woman would sway back as if she really were riding him. Since March, it was the same woman over and over, a redhead. In the morning, before I was called to breakfast, they'd be dressing and the man would slap the woman's behind and then they'd hug. Both would have just shirts on and their behinds would smile shyly at the window.

Now that the man was on the porch where everyone could see him he became a curiousity. From time to time he'd put down his paper and watch us and we would interrupt our game to watch him from across the street. We played in the Hudson's front yard because they had one. On our side the hill was steeper and even the little square of lawn sloped from the front porch right down to the sidewalk and then a thin rectangle of grass before the street. The Hudson's side was flatter—a plateau before the hill fell away behind their house.

And the Hudson's didn't care. They didn't have kids except for little Marie, who was only two. She sat on the front walk like somebody's doll bundled and chubby and we just had to make sure she didn't crawl off somewhere while we played Tag or Hopscotch or Duck Duck Goose. These were silly kid games but we never did anything differently since everybody except Tina was younger than me and they had the numbers.

So we played Duck Goose Goose with little Marie burbling in the center and Tommy Nelson whacking our heads as he went by saying, "Duck, duck, duck, duck..." and he would go round and round, full up with his own power to circle us, hitting and hitting, until someone would say, "C'mon, Tommy," and his next trip around he'd smack that person a good one and shout, "Goose!" and go tearing off into the double hedge that separated the Hudson's from the professor's house next door. And all that while I sat with my legs double-backed, my hind end bones on my heels, my knees in the cool new grass and I wondered about the man on the porch and I was certain he was watching us, too. When my back was to him, I felt his eyes go down my ponytail. When I sat facing him, I was never sure when he looked up from his paper if his gaze was into the intersection down the block, or into the heart of me.

One Saturday late in May when I realized summer was coming and I was apprehensive because I didn't want to go diving and I didn't want to spend all my free time babysitting Jeremy and little Marie and the Nelson twins, Tommy and Daniel, and who knew who else—the Kosner kid and Laurie Breckner and Arnold Moovly and anyone else ten years or younger for three blocks around—the man with the newspaper was without his paper. The sun heated us under our shirts, had been since morning, and we were now in swimsuits with t-shirts on top. We were taking turns with the hose and running through the sprinklers; I'd also wrested Jeremy's X-ray squirt gun from him and was dousing him with that, my hand locked tight on his wrist, but with exasperation and not real joy.

From across the street I could hear the sound of stones plunking on wood.

The man had a wood board on the stoop next to him and he was placing one stone after another on the board, pausing, his fingers to his lips, and then placing another. Plunk, plunk, hollowly from across the street. I let go of the squealing Jeremy, thrust his gun back into his surprised hands and stalked off, bits of wet grass clinging to my ankles.

"Hey," Jeremy called and I heard him wince Ai, ai, ai, as he short-footed his way across the street.

I pretended to go into the house for a towel and came back out, rubbing my hair and watching over the short hedge between our houses as the man worked his stones, black ones and white ones, into patterns on a grid-covered board, then shook his head and separated the stones into two piles with his fingers.

What's that? I wanted to know and then realized I'd spoken aloud.

You want to play? He squinted, his eyes far back in his head. Smiling, the wispy ends of his mustache touched his teeth.

I rubbed my hair, considering. Oh, all right, I said just before Jeremy bolted down our steps, his lips spraying Schure! ahead of him. He ran anyway.

"My name's Fred," the man said.

Jeremy panted, "I'm Jeremy and she's Stephanie."

"How do you do?" Fred said.

I shrugged, as if I were indifferent to being fine or not. Jeremy said he was great and offered his bicep to prove it.

Fred nodded and motioned at the board. "Want to learn?" he asked me. "I'm always looking for competition."

Jeremy said, "I'll watch" and plopped himself on the step below Fred as if he were a part of the game. His head toggled back and forth eagerly. "How come you're always home so fast?"

"I'm a landscape architect. Do you know what that is? I design the outsides of buildings—what kind of trees and grass the bushes and flowers get planted. And so Leon doesn't get lonely—" here Leon looked up from the stick he was disintegrating and Fred shook his head and Leon went back to gnawing "—I draw lots of these outsides at home."

He was talking to Jeremy and me as if we were the same age, but he was looking at me as if I were older, older even than I was. When the next breeze came by I felt the goosebumps and I decided I didn't like him.

But then he asked me what it was I did as if I did something and before I could think I said, "I'm going to be a diver," and Jeremy piped in his "In the Olympicth!" and I aimed a kick at Jeremy's instep and Fred laughed and suddenly everything was natural and he took the stones and showed me how the game was played, like tic-tac-toe, he said, only you play on the crossings, where the lines meet, not in the boxes, and you have to get five in a row, not three, and the whole game's bigger, of course, because you have all this area to play with. And so we started playing and he patiently explained my mistakes and won graciously and said he wouldn't give me any freebies but it was only a matter of time before I'd be able to beat him and sometime during those games—each took fifteen minutes or so—Jeremy got bored and went back to the sprinkler and the kids his age and we were left there, Fred and I, his index finger pressed to his lips, my hands cupping my chin and all and everything seemed concentrated on that wooden board, the world divided very cleanly into white stones and black stones.

Dinnertime came and my mother stepped outside and without so much as glancing over to where I was shouted in that sing-song voice she used when she was tired, "JEreMY! STEphanIE!" the first and last syllables of our names coming out strong and shrill and making me wince because it was as if we were cattle being called into the barn and usually it was that way, Jeremy and I heading up the steps with a longing backward glance at whatever game we'd had to leave.

But I didn't go this time because I was winning the game. I could sense that I was making Fred put his black stones down where he had to, where I wanted him to, not where he did and I was smiling as I put the final piece down click! and he couldn't do anything but smile too and say, "You've just learned Five Stone."

My mother was on the porch again, not looking, shrill, "STEphanIE!" and I said I'd be back tomorrow and he nodded in that way adults nod to each other, and nothing, not even my parents' evening wrangle could undo the feeling I got from that nod.

I told my parents I did want to learn diving with Gordon Gordon. He picked me up every morning at eight and worked with me and another dozen boys and girls my age until one o'clock. Jeremy and the others still got around by carpool and I didn't see them till later, since the diving lessons were given at the Seberg Community Pool, a pool with lane lines and chlorinated water. My mother wasn't carpooling anymore. Over the winter she'd gotten her realtor's license and then bought a white MG sports car with a black interior. She'd be gone most of the day with clients, showing houses, looking at property, arranging money. She'd come home just in time to put dinner on, or she'd come home tired and Jeremy and I would eat sandwiches and my parents would have their martini and go out to eat later. I had a regular job now babysitting little Marie. I'd come home from diving, change into dry clothes and my mother would be polishing off a late lunch of cottage cheese and pineapple. She was suddenly concerned about her figure. She'd spend ages in front of the hall mirror, checking her profile, one hand pressing on her tummy, the fingers spread out, as if she could hold back any bulge with a little hand pressure. One night I heard from behind their closed bedroom door my mother grunting with sharp exhalations, "I won't be fat! I won't be fat!"

My father said, "Jesus, Laurie, you're not fat."

"So what's this?" my mother demanded. I imagined her pausing in mid-situp and grabbing two handfuls of belly.

"Handles," my father chuckled. "So I get a better grip."

"Fuck you," my mother said. "You should be doing some of these yourself."

On Saturdays and Sundays when it was sunny my mother took a romance novel and a big beach blanket and lay out on the front walk above the steps in a too-small aqua bikini. Every summer before she'd worn maillots. The bikini was awful. The situps or whatever she performed at night hadn't taken yet and her belly flesh was still soft and rumpled-looking. She was short, too, and the two pieces of her suit stretched as if their intent was to hold together three dissimilar rounds of flesh.

She knew what I was thinking as I sat reading the funnies, I with my long coltish legs and flat stomach and breasts yet unaware of gravity and I could tell she blamed my figure for hers, as if I were directly responsible for a belly that touched earth before her bust. I was kept out of the house as much as possible, as if my presence were a reproach. She arranged with the Hudsons my afternoons with little Marie. She called me back to dinner as if it were an unwanted obligation for her to feed me. Her voice swelled with resignation. My father came home at five-thirty driving the station wagon and she addressed him as if he were in on it, too—this conspiracy of husband and offspring to mottle her with cellulite and wrinkles.

In late June my mother burned a pot roast which we did our best to eat but couldn't and finally my father said, let's get some pizza and my mother looked at each of us sullenly and then burst into tears, and heels of her hands pressed into her eye sockets and my father ushered us from the room and said for us to wash our dishes. I put the food aside in a tupperware container for Leon and over the running water I could hear their voices, my father saying, What's wrong, Laurie? What's happened? and my mother saying, Nothing, over and over and breathing hard intakes of breath confused with sobs, her breathing tangled, and finally sorting it out and saying, It's nothing, really, and my father taking my mother upstairs and then coming down alone and saying with forced brightness, How 'bout some pizza, huh? and so we went but things were different, they'd been different all summer and the next day I asked Fred about it because he'd know better than anyone and could tell me.

"Something's wrong with my mother," I told him.

He shrugged. "It's just a phase, Stephers. Everyone goes through phases."

"I don't know," I said. "I suppose."

We were sitting on his second floor deck with the five stone board between us. He was thinking about his next move. I already had him—crossed threes—but he wasn't conceding yet. I tossed a stone up and clapped my hands around it, frightening a bird who'd been perched on the pipe railing watching us. It was like I was catching my own heart. Out loud I said, "My mother doesn't like me."

"That's a phase you're going through."

"She really doesn't."

Fred straightened and sighed. He started flicking his stones towards his side of the board. "You always do it when you're supposed to be on defense," he said. "It's time you learned the more complicated game, so I can start winning again. You want a soda?"

He stood and we heard a Yoo hoo! from below. It was the red-haired woman, Marilyn. I'd seen her and heard Fred mention her, but we hadn't met. I leaned over the railing to look. She was all curls and her jeans were crease-ironed. Pale lipstick and freckles. Shorter than Fred, but the right height.

"You're off early," Fred said.

"And none too soon. I see you already have a woman up there."

She came up and Fred introduced us and got drinks for both of them and a coke for me. She squatted to shake my hand and orange curls swung off her shoulders and danced. I felt the tug of my braid, the dull plait of it, the rubber-band marking where the split ends started. Marilyn stood, laced her hands on Fred's shoulder and rested her chin there and gazed at him with what had to be love.

"I was just about to teach Stephers how to play Go," he explained.

"But that takes so long," Marilyn said in the whine Jeremy often used to get his way.

Fred checked his watch. Marilyn batted her wide green eyes. I sipped my soda, my lips tingling.

"Just to show her—" he said to Marilyn.

I set my glass by my heel and rose, saying, I should go, hoping Fred would say, No, wait, we'll just take a minute, but he didn't, he took Marilyn's fingers in his own and said, That one, you know, if she were eight, ten years older— and Marilyn said, I know, and punched him high on the shoulder and I skipped down the stairs inside his house, my cheeks hot and then I was outside with them above and behind me and my braid went thop thop on my back and my cheeks still burned and I thought Why not?

Diving, Gordon Gordon said, is a listless activity, performed by a finely tuned body. To do it right, you must believe the dive is already done and you are climbing from the water, bored with your own body's perfection. The dive must be so natural, so commonplace, that you could fall asleep in the middle of it and no one would notice. Not even yourself, until the water wakes you.

Gordon Gordon talked a great dive.

But for all Gordon's talking to the contrary, terror still had tiny claws deep in my back. "You must relax," Gordon said, "when you don't think you are more flawless than anyone here." He had me bend double on the high board and grab my ankles with my hands, my knees locked. Then he wedged his heel between my buttocks and shoved. The object was for me to straighten out and land perfectly extended—toes pointed, back arched, pectorals prominent, eyes level, looking upside down at the world. Usually his push sent me tumbling, sprawling all over the place, and frantically I'd try to right myself. If I didn't the splat was fearsome. I'd ache clear to the small of my back, the whole front of me feeling slapped.

"You must learn to recover," Gordon Gordon said. "You must learn to land."

I think Gordon Gordon liked planting his foot on my buttocks. I think he took some small thrill out of feeling me up with his toes. I learned to hate him.

The breathing exercises, the running, the kickboards, the lingering of his instep on the curve of my rump, the cold smell of metal and chlorine on your neck as he talked you through each new dive (so close your ear felt the explosion of his breath), I learned to hate all of it. What kept me going was that I couldn't not go. Also, I really did want to learn the one dive that most terrified and thrilled me. I believed him about that.

Most of what he said about the other dives I'd tell Fred about later, how he made us act out everything on the grass, rolling and twisting on our backs on the dry ground, tumbling through gainers, half-gainers, somersaults and flips, and his telling us, There is no ground! There is no ground! You're alone in the air, a creature falling! And we'd laugh and laugh.

But for this dive Gordon Gordon had us sit in a semi-circle on the grass, and on the edge of the pool he trundled out a chalkboard. In one gracious stroke he drew the most beautiful arc. That's it, he said. You launch yourself into empty space—it's not like any other dive, where mutliple gyrations earn you points—and then you arch down. Just like that, he said, and drew another arc. Again, it was beautiful.

I took to skipping days when I knew we'd be working on tucks and somersaults, since those came to me surprisingly easy—I just kept my eyes closed and pretended I was playing with Jeremy and Tina and the Nelson twins and when I finished the water was there; I only had time to be briefly shocked before I plunged into clear blue and it was over.

It was on one of those days I skipped, a warm bright July morning that seemed too hospitable to spend diving into chilly water again and again, that I found out about my mother. I skipped days by waiting curbside till Gordon Gordon came, my mother off in her MG minutes before, my father off in the station wagon a good half-hour before that, and I'd tell Gordon Gordon I had to spend the whole day babysitting little Marie Hudson and I was sorry, but I'd work doubly hard tomorrow—we were going to be working on the swan, weren't we?—and I'd even practice twists and such on the ground, I promised. He'd roll his window back up and off he'd go and I'd have the morning to think about my life with Fred. I'd think about being old enough to displace Marilyn. I'd take her hands off his shoulder and tell her she wasn't wanted anymore and Fred would nod agreement, a slight smile under his brown mustache and poof! she'd be gone as if she'd never existed and Fred and I would eat some jam and toast and go shopping and play long games of Go we'd take turns winning, and we would spend time at the beach and he would watch me make perfect swan dives—I really could fly but I'd let myself fall just for the beauty of it. Fred would clap his hands once and dry me off and shyly then the other things would happen. I couldn't think about them but I'd get all quivery thinking about wearing his shirts in the morning and that one friendly slap that'd catch me under my shirt tail and I think I'd look very good in one of his shirts, yes, with my long legs and full thighs and just the whisper of my behind visible when I walked away from him to make our breakfast.

My mother came back then, I recognized the sound of her MG, the throaty grumbling of it from over the hill. It was ten in the morning and I was sitting on the steps and I scampered into the house afraid she'd find me skipping and really light into me so I hid in my room, ready to crawl into the closet. My shoes were off and I heard the door open and her laugh and her say, Just a minute, Paul, and the refrigerator opened and I could almost hear it hum I was listening so hard and a bottle clinked out and she said, I was saving this for a day like today and a man's voice not my father's said, All right, little lady, and then they were giggling, for christ's sake, like a couple of kids. The door opened and closed and I rushed to the window but all I saw was my mother's familiar small bulk and the deep gray back and white shirt collar peeking above that and the black back of the head of someone a good eight inches taller than my mother and the green bottle flashing white in the sun and tree branches obscured them then. And then they were in the car and the car roared back to life and they were gone and I sat on the bed with one leg pulled underneath my heinie where Gordon Gordon placed his foot and I kept thinking not my father not my father not my father.

Jeremy came home then only it was hours later and my knee hurt from being bent that way so long. The door slammed and I came downstairs. Jeremy was in the kitchen. I'm going to watch little Marie, I said, and Jeremy nodded, engrossed in his peanut butter and jelly. Only I didn't go there. Let Mrs. Hudson watch her own kid, I thought. I had Fred's key, he'd given it to me to walk Leon if I wanted to. Leon didn't need the walk, usually he could wait so I never did, out of fear, I guess, being in Fred's house like that but now I did. I unlocked the door and Leon bounded down from upstairs with the half-chewed cardboard tube of a t.p. roll in his mouth, his tail wagging. He didn't even bark. You belong here, his tail said and I got the leash from the downstairs bureau but only held it in my hand. Let's go, I said and Leon was out the door, his nails clicking, his tail plumed high and happy.

The quaking aspen behind the houses quaked silver and every leaf on the other trees shuddered. I wanted to run but where? They could be in the park. But I can't go there, I'd spend all my time looking and praying not to find. At the playground would be a lot of kids dumber than Jeremy who'd make a big fuss over Leon and even though I'd be ignored I'd still have to be there so after a few blocks I crossed the street and walked back. I wasn't even sure if Leon had done his duty.

Fred's Go board was on his coffee table with the wooden boxes of stones next to it. The stones looked like M&M's washed clean. I played a long game of five-stone by myself. Then another and another. I would have liked to have played Go but I didn't know enough about it yet. Fred said it was really a simple game with delicate intricacies but I saw it only as maddeningly complex. The board stretched immensely. I couldn't imagine trying to fill it all up though that was what I was doing playing five-stone. I blundered again and again against myself, filling up the center of each pattern with stupid moves when after I reflected a moment the best moves were to the outside, off in almost empty space where they controlled play but didn't grubbily jostle for position against all the other stones.

What could I possibly say to my mother?

She was home by mid-afternoon, weaving a bit in her pumps but home anyway, a small bag of groceries clutched to her chest. I kept playing five-stone. I wanted to go back to my house and sit on a high stool by the counter and ask her how her day went and watch her put away the groceries. I wanted her to mutter something stupid about the price of broccoli and then ask her who's Paul, anyway, and watch the milk jug bounce off the floor but then I realized that was a helpless stupid thing to do, something Jeremy would do. What I wanted was for my mother to say to me I know what you're thinking and it's not true and for her to say it with such finality and honesty that I believed her but I didn't think I could believe her about anything again. And then Fred was sitting next to me on the sofa, I hadn't even heard him come in and he said, So what is it, Stephers? and I sobbed, Oh, Fred, and broke in his astonished arms and Leon scratched my legs pawing to see what was the matter. It stung but I kept crying and Fred kept saying, Hey, hey, it's okay as if he were cheering for me. Behind me he was directing Marilyn to get me some iced tea and red juice—that was what they called the exlixir of Benedryl—and he made me swallow one and then the other and I hated myself for being the center of all this attention and finally I calmed down and took whole breaths.

Fred had me lay down on the couch, a red leather couch I stuck to even though it felt cool to my hands, and he went next door.

My mother stood behind the couch looking very tired, I could see how her skin especially around the cheekbones had lost the tautness mine had and she said quietly looking at my puffy red eyes You didn't go swimming today, did you? and I didn't answer but we both knew what we knew and my mother trying to smile said to Fred, Growing pains and a case of the guilts, as if I did this all the time and Fred smiled as if he agreed. I hated him for that and wondered if they'd worked something out between them over at our house, one of those hushed conversations adults have that are held so we know they're being held but don't quite know why. I tried to imagine my mother with this man smiling over me and somehow I pictured it, my mother's small breasts and lumpy belly being handled by Fred's sure hands and her shortness and his length coming together, him riding her like a popsicle stick balanced on a doughnut and I wanted to laugh but my throat felt scummy and with Marilyn hovering in the background I saw how everything was lost. Then I was taken home and put to bed and given more red juice and told to come down when I felt better and I didn't feel better until the morning when the sun coming in fell warm on my chin and thorax and I woke up thinking, All right already.

I didn't see Fred all that much that summer though I continued to let him believe we were friends. He showed me the intricacies of Go, which I became quite good at, and I conceded to him Marilyn's beauty. I spent more time with

Gordon Gordon and took a great interest in the mechanics of each dive. Jeremy and little Marie became only nuisances to be tolerated a few more weeks. I wanted to think that one night my mother would come into my room and sit on the bed, something she never did except when I was sick. I would put down the book I was reading and sit a little higher, arranging my pillows behind me. My mother would pick her words carefully, the tip of her tongue poised on her upper lip, her index finger tracing patterns on the sheet. She would've just finished crying. "What you know about," she would say, "isn't anymore." The words would come out one at a time as if each required its own shallow breath. "I don't think you'll understand," she would say, "but someday—" And her voice would go high there and then come down as if "someday" were a benediction. Instead, my mother took the new distance between us stoically—it was not until much later, until I'd done things I couldn't explain to anyone but myself, that I could understand why she didn't ask me to understand.

The weekend before school started my parents came to the Seberg pool to watch me and Gordon Gordon's other diving pupils go through our paces. Fred and Leon and Marilyn were there, too. Jeremy was home with a cold, which he usually got the weekend before school started in the hopes that it'd turn into pneumonia. It was a blue day with a few passing clouds and a light breeze. The show was pretty routine—mostly o.k. dives, a few botched ones, several scissor-legs that resulted in too much splash, and one belly flop, which received applause anyway, all presided over by Gordon Gordon's tremulous voice, a voice that reverberated over the P.A. like the drone of a far off airplane. After a good dive he'd say, "You'll see that dive this winter at the freshman swim meets," and after a bad dive he'd hurry up and introduce the next person and dive: "Here's Kristy again doing a backwards double somersault" which she would do, more or less o.k., and surface to polite smatters of fingers on palms. We each did seven dives, six all the same and we chose our final one. I got through my dives by thinking of them as patterns executed on the Go board, my body going from gridded point to gridded point and in that manner I avoided the constant terror of being high in the air with a sheet of wobbly board beneath me. I couldn't pretend I was playing with Jeremy and Tina Talperi because it seemed more serious than play. Each dive was marred by what got me through it—a certain jerkiness of the joints as I plotted my body's fall. But at least I didn't screw up any, like almost everyone else did.

Then my last turn came and everyone disappeared. The moment before I could see my parents and Fred and Marilyn and even Leon packed into the portable bleachers opposite me, and then they ceased to exist. The green line of trees behind them receded into nothing. I no longer heard Gordon Gordon and his reedy pronoucement that Stephanie was doing her final dive. The hollow porcelain blue of the water below me and the sky above me vanished. The height was gone. Everything ceased to exist except the slight breeze I felt at my temples and my awareness of my skin and myself inside it, my muscles clean. I took three steps, they could have been from anywhere, from any height, and launched myself: chin up: eyes open, arms back and fluid, legs long and tapering, tapering to where my curled toes seemed pinned against the sky, pinned right there and I would never kiss my shadow.

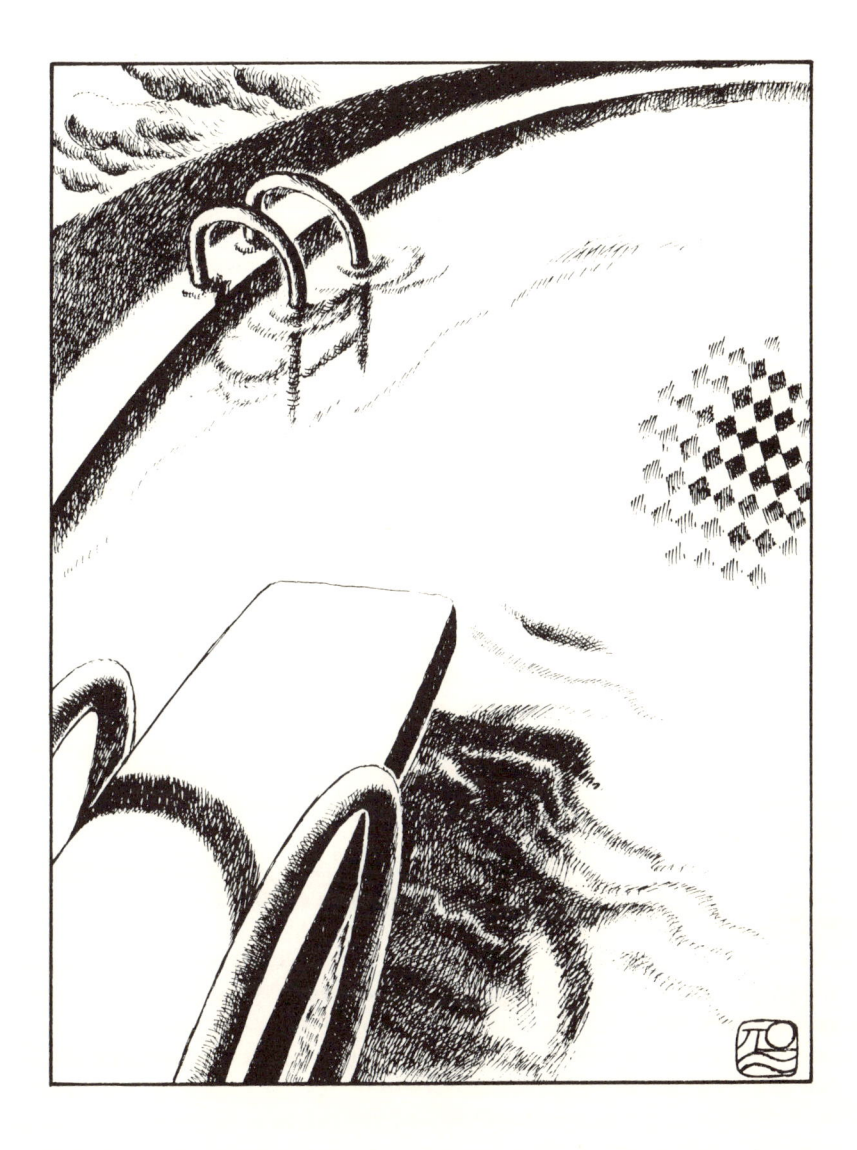

FIXING CARS AND OKLAHOMA

Leonard and Randi became lovers because her car wouldn't start. Leonard was sitting on the front step of his porch sipping a Leinenkugel's and he was watching Randi trying to start her car. It was four o'clock in the afternoon and he'd thought about going to play some basketball at the VFW park but when you've let most of the day slip away like he'd done there's not much point in trying to salvage two hours.

Randi was fed up. It was late August and it was hot and it was even hotter inside her car where the plastic seat cover threatened to cauterize her behind. She did not need a day like this, right after she'd decided she was going to Oklahoma to be a poet. "Oklahoma doesn't have enough poets," she told her boyfriend Mike. "Neither does Rhinelander," Mike told her, "but I'm not one for stopping people from making a fool of themselves wherever they choose to do it." With that she assumed she had his blessing, not that she needed it because she was going anyway, but she wanted to keep on good terms with him in case Oklahoma wasn't what it was cracked up to be.

But today it was hot and her car wouldn't start and there was that guy on his porch across the street watching her struggle and damn it, it was getting to be too much. Where was Oklahoma when you needed it?

She leaned out her window and shouted to Leonard, "I don't suppose you could help a girl? My car won't start."

Leonard was afraid this would happen. He knew one thing about cars: if they didn't start, probably something was wrong. He still had a few swallows left to his Leinie's so he took that with him.

Randi was outside her car already and she had the hood up. Leonard looked around the inside, amazed at how intricate engines has gotten. He'd last owned a car four years ago and it didn't have half the hoses and wires this one had. Finally he found the battery, which was what he was looking for all along, and he said to Randi in his most knowing manner, "I think it's the battery."

"It just grinds and grinds and then there's a clicking noise and then nothing happens," Randi said.

"I know. I was watching," Leonard said. He tipped the long necked bottle and was pleased to remember that what she described was usually the problem with his Pontiac. He almost knew how to fix that.

Randi was relieved to know Leonard'd been watching her. If you're going to have the paranoia of feeling watched, it may as well be true.

"Let me get some tools and I'll be right back. You want a beer?" This woman is cute, Leonard thought. She had a round face and olive skin and shiny black hair halfway down her back. Her eyes were black and sparkly like hard coal behind hugely oval glasses.

"Thanks," Randi said, thinking that life was by no means perfect, but if this guy got her car started it was a step in the right direction.

He came back clutching two Leinie's, an adjustable wrench, a putty knife, a hammer, and a wire brush. Two rags were stuffed in his back pocket. He didn't know why he'd need the hammer, but you could never be sure in these things.

He hummed while he undid the battery cables. He'd never seen this kind before—two plastic bolts that went into the side of the battery. He'd seen enough batteries to know this was a freak of nature. To show he wasn't rattled by this unexpected turn he flashed a smile at her. She was slowly sipping her beer and looking interested. In fact she was checking out his butt while he bent over the engine, but she wasn't inclined to tell him this. No sense complicating your life just because someone fixes your car, especially if it isn't fixed yet.

"Let's see those babies," Leonard said in his best done-this-a-thousand-times tone. Christ, she was cute. Had on this purply-brown leotard that showed off her breasts and a peasant skirt and sandals. Really nice.

The insides of the connectors were crusty green. "Well, this looks like the problem. See this green? Corrosion."

"Is that serious?" she asked, taken by his nicely tanned legs.

"No problem at all," he said, praying silently he did not, in the next few minutes, make an ass of himself.

"This car," she said. "It's been one thing after another. I should just junk it but I need it to get around."

"Strange, though, I haven't seen you around before." He said this and looked both at the space between her breasts and at that which had created the space.

"I started housekeeping for that family down the street. They're from Chicago and just bought the house." She was trying to judge how big he was under his shorts.

"Lot of people from Chicago have houses up here," Leonard said. "It's getting so there're more Chicago people up north than Wisconsinites." He couldn't tell if she was big-hipped or not under that skirt. He was partial to big-hipped women.

"At least in summer," Randi said. She looked down the street so as to give him a profile.

"Oh, they come up for snowmobiling and skiing, too." She purposely gave me that profile, he thought.

"I suppose," Randi said. This guy was skinny, but his arms were tan like his legs and he had a nice butt and he had a face. It wasn't some unshaven mug, and his hair looked good even sweated to his forehead. His nose bent to the left but she had a thing for that. "But let the Chicago people come," she said. "For me it doesn't matter. I'm going to Oklahoma first of September."

"Really? For why?" He wished he smoked; it was the perfect time to light up.

"To write. I'm a poet." That ought to get him, she thought.

"And what might your name be, so years from now I can say I fixed a famous poet's car?" He was pleased he'd worked the question in there like that.

Randi told him and he told her his. He said he's shake but his hands were dirty and she said she understood. Both of them thought they were hitting it off pretty well and they kept the talk going while he worked with the putty knife and wire brush and got everything clean. Then he put the caps back and told her to try it. She did and it caught. Leonard felt the joy of finally getting something right.

Randi's thighs were sweated to the seat but now she didn't care. She asked him if she could buy him a drink for fixing her car. He said fine, could he just change into pants and wash up?

They went to Oxie's on Boom Lake. They sat by the picture window that looked over the lake and they had three screwdrivers apiece. By seven they decided they might as well have dinner, too. Oxie's had great walleye fillet, so that's what they had. Also two more screwdrivers while they watched the sun go down. Seduction City.

Over dinner Randi talked about her life. She had been married once, to an Allis Chalmers tractor heir, but one day she just decided life as a hostess was not her idea of fulfillment, so she just up and left. Just like that, she said, left. She said she'd even loved the guy, but she'd seen one finger bowl too many and that was that. Now she was living with this other guy Mike in a mobile home that wasn't hooked up to water or gas or anything. They were two miles from the main road and the toilet was a shed a hundred yards back of the house. She loved Mike and thought the roughness good for her writing, but Oklahoma had homes with toilets inside. Leonard was going to say so did Wisconsin, but he realized that what she said wasn't what she meant.

He didn't tell her about himself. He didn't say he'd gone to Pembine High School, fifty miles north of nowhere, and had since worked for seven years as a short-order cook at the Y-Go-By in Rhinelander until yesterday, until he got fired for telling Dolores to stuff it up her ass one too many times. It was not his idea of an interesting life. Randi had him all beat for experience. She had a right to say things that weren't quite logical.

Randi asked him for a flashlight after dinner. "Usually I get home before dark," she said. "But I'll need a flashlight tonight to find my way back to the trailer." There was one in her trunk, but he didn't have to know about that. Instead she told him about the night she got lost and twisted her ankle and heard noises that scared her half to death, noises that didn't normally mean a thing.

Leonard said he had one back at his house and when they got there she followed him upstairs.

"Thanks for dinner," he said, handing her the flashlight. She kissed him. The flashlight bounced on the floor. Then they were on the floor.

Later they had two more Leinenkugel's on the porch. It was after two.

"You can keep the flashlight," he said.

"I'll bring it back tomorrow."

"Whenever," Leonard said.

"You did a great job with my car, but I liked you before that."

"It wasn't anything. To tell you the truth the only thing I know about is batteries. If it'd been anything else I couldn't have helped."

"And I wouldn't be here now." They kissed once more and then she went to her car.

A week later Leonard got his flashlight back. Two days after she put Leonard's flashlight in his mailbox Randi made it to Oklahoma and the next time her car broke down she took it to a garage.

"It's a world for head-scratching," Mike would say. But he keeps pretty much to himself these days, so he doesn't get to say it to much of anybody.

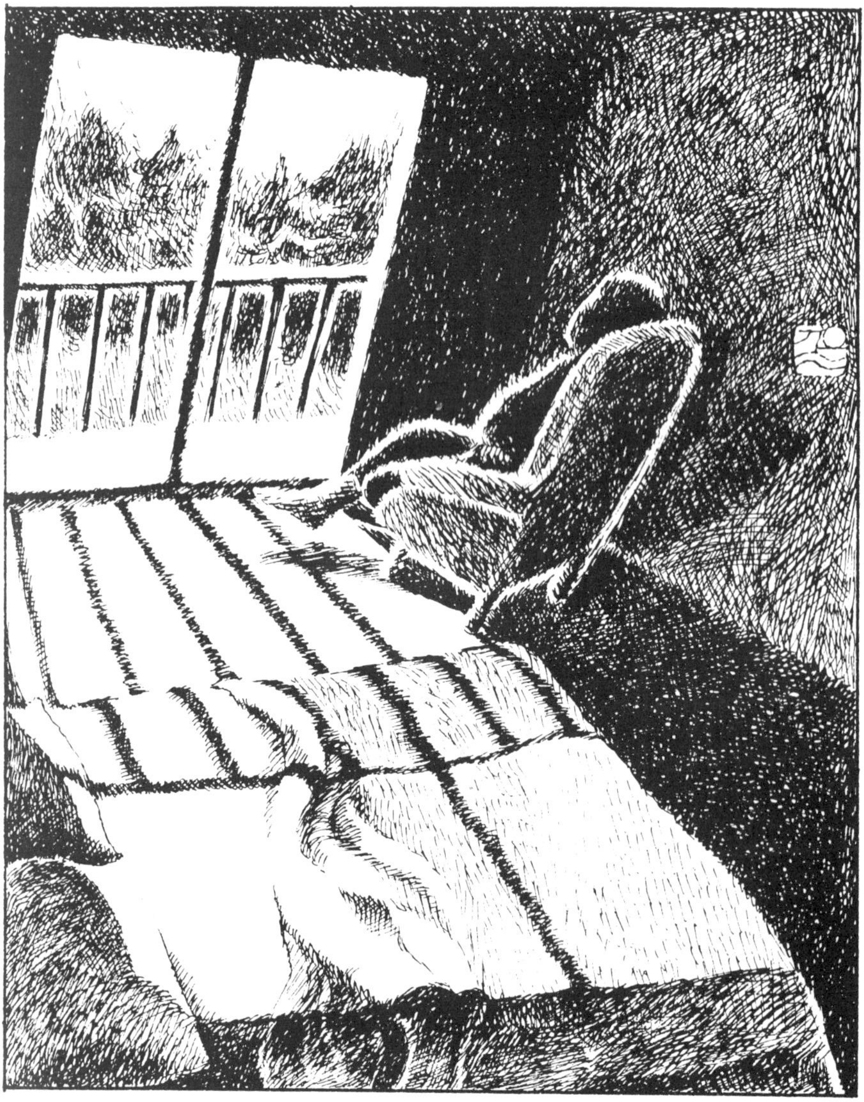

3-D

HONEY, WHAT'S THAT?

It was mid-October. My wife and I were having a difficult time of it.
"What's wrong?" I asked her one night.
"Nothing," she told me.
I knew she was lying.
I took a shower and we got ready for bed. As she undressed in the bathroom I watched the pattern of shadow that ran across our bed and onto the wall. Off our bedroom was a small enclosed balcony, and the streetlights cast the shadow of the wrought iron railing onto the sheets. We'd never gotten curtains for the sliding glass door. The door was double-paned so the shadow had a ghost, an inch apart from the first shadow, and amber colored. I didn't know why the second shadow was amber colored, but it was. I was sitting in a chair with a towel draped over my lap in front of the window.
My wife came into the room in her panties. Her shoulders looked white and thin. From her bureau she took a blue t-shirt. She pulled that on and got in bed. She picked up the book she'd been reading and lit a cigarette. Her eyes pinched together as she read.
"You shouldn't read without a light on," I said.
"I'm only going to read for a little while."
"What happened today at the office?" I asked. "I tried to reach you, but they said you were out."
"Nothing. Rob and I had a long lunch." Rob was a new assistant buyer my wife worked with. They put him in her cubicle, so they usually went to lunch at the same time.
"What did you talk about?"

"Look at that," she said, pointing at the wall. The shadow of my shoulders and head grew out of the shadow of her torso. The shadow of the smoke floated between our heads.

"Isn't that strange?" she said. "You should take a picture of that."

"Do we have any film?" I said. "I think we finished off that last roll at your parents."

"Oh," she said, and looked down at her book.

"Did Rob say anything interesting today?"

"The usual."

"What's that?" I said.

"What's what?"

"The usual?"

She lit another cigarette. "Aren't you going to get that wet towel off?"

"I was just thinking," I said. "There's something wrong, isn't there?"

"Will you please stop asking me that?"

"But there's something wrong."

"Nothing is wrong. Nothing."

"Why don't you tell me what's bothering you?"

She closed her book and put out the cigarette. "Come to bed. You make me nervous sitting there like that."

I went into the bathroom and brushed my teeth. When I came back out she was lying down, facing the picture window, but with her eyes closed. I settled into bed behind her. My arm came over her waist and I rested my hand inside her t-shirt on the flat of her stomach.

"Honey, what's that?" she said.

"What's what?" I lifted my head.

"What's that outside the window?"

"Where?"

"Outside. On the balcony. I heard someone."

"There's no one out there."

"No. I heard it. Something is out there."

"If anyone was out there we'd see his shadow."

"You better look. I think someone is out there."

I got out of bed. I slid the door open and stepped out. A slight breeze stirred a few leaves. They skittered across the weathered wood. Cold ran up my legs.

Nothing was out there. She was lying again.

NEVER AGAIN

"No," he tells me. "It didn't happen like that."
He's just come in. I'm still dressed, lying on the bed with a light on. I'm feeling tired and angry and disgusted and lots of other things it wouldn't do any good to mention. Last week I turned thirty-seven and that night he turned on Johnny Carson. Tonight I don't know who he turned on, but it's damn near three.
"We were just talking," he tells me.
"Just talking," I say.
"We had some wine. I lost control."
"You could've called."
"I was drunk. I wasn't thinking."
"It would be different," I say, "if this were the first time."
"Never again."
I reach for my cigarettes.
"I'm not the kind of person you want to talk to anymore."
"What do you mean?" he says. "You're a great listener." He sits on the bed next to me and pulls off his shoes.
"You're bored with me." I'm looking at the wall across from the bed. I light a cigarette and smoke drifts across the lampshade.
"I can imagine the other ones," he says. "They'll all be you."
"You may as well be with them then."
"Come on. Worse things have happened to us." His finger plays with my earlobe.
"Not over and over again."
His finger draws a line from my ear down my neck and under my chin. I stare at the end of my cigarette.
"Never again." He kisses the tip of my nose.
"I really wish I could believe you."
"You can." His tongue is in my ear. I take a long drag and let the smoke reach me everywhere inside.
"It can't keep on like this."
"Like what?" He's undoing my blouse.
"These conversations."
"What conversations?" He takes the cigarette from me, puts it in the ashtray, and turns out the light. His breath is warm on my stomach.

BOXERS

It rang a long time before she answered.
"Melanie? This is Paul."
"Paul? Oh, Paul. From the laundromat."
She made it sound like he worked there. He didn't—it was just that Alice's Norge was on the fritz again and Melanie'd been out of detergent.
"You said I should call you."
"My husband's home."
"Your husband?"
"My husband—Jack."
"Oh. Jack."
"You knew I was married, didn't you?"
"Yeah, I guess."
"You helped take his underwear out of the dryer."
"I guess I wasn't looking."
"I take it your wife isn't home."
"My wife?" Alice and he weren't married. They'd been living together for ten months and except for the last two they'd been talking about getting married. But Alice wasn't so sure anymore and so he wasn't either.
"I noticed her clothes when you were folding," Melanie said.
"Oh. Well, she said she was going shopping," Paul said. Let it ride, he thought. No point in explaining about Alice. Alice was a dead letter.
"This will have to be short. Jack's on the patio barbecuing, but he could come in any time."
"Maybe I should call my you back later."
"No, you keep talking. I'll just hang up if he comes in."
"So what about getting together sometime? Late afternoon maybe?" That didn't sound nearly as definite as he'd wanted. "Like you suggested," he added, hoping it would help.
"Jack works at night," Melanie said. "He's home all day."
"How about after he leaves?"
"He comes home early in the morning."
"For Christ's sake, I'm not talking about the whole night! Just a few drinks. Couldn't we go out and have a few drinks?" He caught himself. He was nearly shouting. Perhaps he had. Lord, this was turning out badly. Complete turnaround from yesterday. She sounded bored.
She said, "What about your wife?"

He wanted to scream, "She's not my wife!" But instead he said, "She's always gone in the evenings. Visiting friends."

"Could you hold just a minute? I have to freshen my drink."

He heard the bump of the phone being put down and wondered what he'd do if Jack picked it up. He thought about yesterday. He'd just closed the lids on his and Alice's clothes. Water hissed underneath and he was about to go outside for a smoke when Melanie introduced herself and asked would he mind spotting her some detergent, she only had enough money for the wash and dry. He gave her two cups of Tide and after her clothes were going they stepped out for a cigarette. He ended up not smoking. He kept lighting cigarettes for her and they talked through both cycles.

Outside they watched the stars come out. He said you could never see them as well as in the city as you do in the country and she said that's probably true. Their dryers clunked off and while they folded and stacked they talked about getting together and how crazy it was—them, the laundromat—just like in the T.V. commercials. He got her phone number and she said, Please do call me. He gave her a kiss on the cheek and she smiled.

"Are you still there, Paul?"

"When can I see you, Melanie?"

"Look, I really don't want to start anything. It was just for laughs, okay?"

He didn't know what to say to her.

Then she was screaming, "Stop it! Do you hear me? Stop it! Stop that!" Then he heard, farther away, as if from another room, "It's him again, honey," and then a man's voice saying something. A moment's silence and he knew he should hang up, but he didn't.

Then Jack's voice was in his ear, very calm, as if Jack were an FM music-of-your-life announcer. "Look, buddy, I know how it is. She met you at the laundromat, right? Or the grocery store. It's nothing, she does it all the time. For kicks, see? It doesn't mean anything because she can't help herself. She gets on a jag and then forgets it, but by then some clown like you is all hung up. Do yourself a favor, buddy, and forget it ever happened." Then the line went dead. Paul took a long breath and put the phone down.

That night he watched the late show and cleaned the apartment. Alice still wasn't home. He started setting out the clothes he'd wear the next day. In his bureau he found a pair of Jack's underwear that had gotten mixed in with his own while he and Melanie were folding. He undressed except for his socks and put on Jack's underwear: green paisley boxers, size forty. Ridiculously huge. They barely held at his hips and the bottom of the shorts were over his knees.

He looked at himself in the mirror. He turned this way and that. Then he started to do the Twist. At first he held the boxers up with one hand, and then he let go.

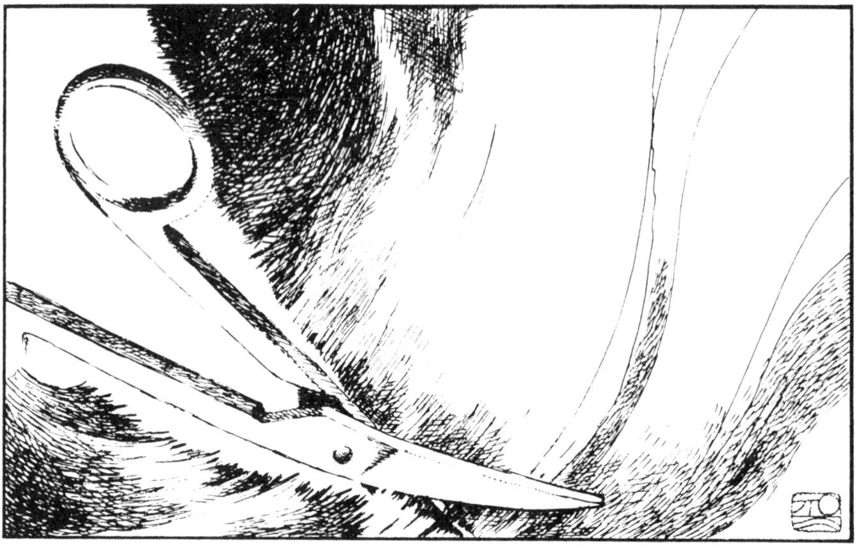

LAKE POYGAN
AND THE POLITICS OF DEPARTURE

It was a day in March, last Thursday to be exact, when the mud froze and the fog and cold were such that if there wasn't mud to freeze you'd swear it was November. Weston and I got drunk that night and while walking home on streets greasy with frost we decided that as soon as we got a sunny day of sixty degrees we'd go swimming.

This Saturday it gets up to sixty and the sun is out. While we eat our eggs I tell Weston a promise is a promise.

Weston says, "We're gonna freeze our balls, Karla."

"Only one of us," I say.

I pour coffee for each of us and while I read the morning paper Weston smears jelly on my toes and starts licking it off. One thing leads to another.

"Wes," I say, "we're going swimming later, save your strength."

"Karla," he says, "I need to get my blood moving or that lake will claim its next victim." He's joking, of course. It's been seven years since Lake Poygan had a winter drowning, and that was only because a snowmobiler went across it in early March when any fool knows the ice is soft as plastic.

About two hours later we have a shower and start packing for the lake. Towels, change of clothes, bottle of Taylor wine, bottle of Old Grand Dad, big blanket, frisbee, picnic basket, etc.

"You think we should tell somebody where we're going?" Weston asks. "Just in case?"

"Don't be silly, Wes. We'll jump in and out. Like the polar bear people, only not so crazy."

"March is crazy enough for me," Weston says. "When are we going to move to some sunshine?"

"Wes," I say. "You know I'm not the one to say when we're moving." Weston is a writer and has been working on this screenplay for a couple of years now. Frankly, though, he doesn't work on it that much. I don't think he's gotten more than three pages done this whole winter. If it weren't for the fact that he'd shrivel and die without me I'd have said years ago that he wasn't worth sticking around for.

We live in Poy Sippi, in the heart of a big lake region. "More lakes than you can shake a stick at," my father would say. Weston's from California, though, and lately he's been pressing for us to get back out there, or anyplace where it's warm all year. He's chomping at the bit after two winters in Wisconsin, and they were mild winters at that. He's going on this swim outing only because he wants to prove he can do it—that he wants to leave only out of preference, not because of a lack of guts, as he knows my father suspects.

My father was never too keen on Weston in the first place. Weston looks and dresses like "one of those California freaks"—Weston's a Leo and wears a pewter lion on a silver chain around his neck—to put the idea in my father's head, and for my father, once an idea is there, it's there, and no, thank you, ma'am, I'll keep to that. It didn't help Weston any to ask my father what sign he was. Weston said he wanted to find out if my father and he were going to get along. My father said he wouldn't need a zodiac to figure that one out.

Weston's been saying once his script is done we should go to Hollywood to peddle it and I said fine, but it's got to be finished first. I know I'll like California as much as the next person, but I'm not going anywhere unless I've got a reason, and my going out to California with Weston to support him while he thinks about maybe writing a movie isn't my idea of a good reason.

His movie of late has gotten to be a sore point between us. I only ask him anymore when he starts acting like a slug, assuming I'll do everything: the cooking, the cleaning, the bread-winning and the bill-paying, and then make sweet love with him all night long, which isn't going to happen.

Weston's movie is supposed to be about us—autobiographical, Weston calls it. I don't like that idea, but Weston once wrote a story about me cleaning some fish he'd caught that got published in *Fishing Facts* magazine, so I guess he knows what he's doing.

I'm the one supporting us, though. I've got a job at Pfelter's at the checkout. It's good enough for rent (which we pay to my father since we live in a house he foreclosed on) and for groceries, and I've even managed to put away a tidy sum without telling Weston. Weston still has some pharmaceutical habits that I dropped when we were talking about maybe someday having a family, and if Weston knew about my pin money he'd be into it quick as a snake sucks eggs.

Weston tells me I don't understand that writing isn't a nine-to-five job. He tells me I have no imagination. I remind him of Thomas Edison and inspiration/perspiration. I tell him he doesn't have to sweat blood, I'd just like to see him working on something. Weston packs his pipe from the tray he keeps under the easy chair and says he's always working, he's just not writing it down. "I'm not print-oriented," he says. And I say, "Well, that's a very nice sentence you just concocted, Wes, but it's gone now forever unless you write it down this minute," and he says, "It'll come, it'll come," and I say, "Just let me know when it gets here, okay, so we can get a move on ourselves."

Just to change the subject I tell Weston it looks like he could use a haircut. He knows I don't mean a real haircut, it's just that the ends are getting real splintery and I could nip that off for him so it will still be long but look better. Weston has wonderful blond hair. With his brown beard he looks like Jesus. I tried drawing him once, but he came out looking thin and Oriental, not like himself at all.

Weston says if he lets me cut his hair, could we make a day of it and not go to the lake? I give him a look and he knows it's going to be both, not a pick and choose. He scowls and says, "Get the scissors, but remember, not too much."

I say it'll only take a minute and then we can go to the lake. By then the sun will be going full blast.

Weston says, "The sun's never going full blast here."

"Hush, Wes," I say. "Neither are you."

"I've got a furnace all right," he says. "But the cold here has just about knocked out my pilot light. How can anyone think, let alone work, when you're constantly wondering if you'll ever see spring again?"

"This is spring, Wes. It's sixty degrees, for God's sake."

I get the scissors from the bathroom. They're tiny fingernail trimming scissors I use for just about everything. I start by wetting down his hair. The sun has brightened the room and Wes's hair is blond like wheat when the sun's out after a thunderstorm. He doesn't have thick hair so in a minute it's plastered to his forehead, his ears, and the back of his neck. I have always been fond of the shape of Weston's head.

"We'll have a relapse of piss-poor winter, you can count on it," he says and relights his pipe.

"You're not smoking that stuff in my kitchen," I say. I don't like that stuff anymore, and Weston knows it. We've come to words over it several times. Weston sets the pipe on the drainboard. I'm still combing his hair, straight and wet like a dog's. I follow the comb with my fingers. Then I start cutting. "You know, Wes, I wouldn't mind being in California by summer."

"I'm all for that," he says. "Summer's a good time."

I'm taking maybe an inch off all the way around. I twist his hair up by the ends. Snip, snip and move on.

"You know," Weston says, "this would be a good scene for my movie. You know, something common but touching. Something the audience can relate to."

"How do *you* like it?" I ask him. "Are you relating?"

Weston reaches a hand up and touches my wrist. "I like it fine," he says. I go on cutting.

"Summer in California," Weston says. "I can't wait. You'll get a job, I'll write on the beach—"

I snip a lock of hair off very close to Weston's ear. Weston knows this is a warning, but he pays it no heed.

"Be careful," he says. "I don't want to look like Ed."

Ed's my father. My father has a crew cut.

With one bite of the scissors I gouge out a width of hair a foot shorter than anyplace else. Weston whirls.

"What did you do?" he screams.

In my hands I hold twelve inches of hair that used to be in the back of Weston's beautiful head. I look at it like somebody else put it there, but I have one of those smiles on my face.

"Oh, my God!" Weston bolts for the bathroom. I hear him wailing from in there. "My God, Karla, what have you done? Sweet Christ, you've raped my head!"

I come into the bathroom. "I'll even it off," I say.

"You had to cut enough so I couldn't hide it, didn't you?" he says. "I was joking, for Christ's sake. Joking, you understand? Can't you take a joke?"

"It's not that bad," I say. "I'll work around it and it'll be okay. It won't look anything like Ed's."

"Why didn't you just hit me or something?"

I pat his shoulder. "I lost my head, Wes. I'll make it up to you." He can tell I'm not sincere. We go back to the kitchen and I recut everything to its new length.

"I look stupid," he says when I'm done. "I'm a blond Prince Valiant."

He's right. He looks like he's wearing a German helmet. "I'll trim some more," I say.

Weston reaches for the drainboard. "I'm going to need another bowl for this."

I decide not to argue with him about it. I don't know what I'm going to do, but it's not going to be arguing. Arguing wears me out. I go into work and feel like hell. I look like death warmed over, and everyone can tell I've been arguing with Weston. In Poy Sippi everyone knows the cause of everything. "She's been arguing with Wes, that lump of a husband," they're saying. "And she's pretty, too," they add. And I *am* pretty. It's just that I don't have time to look that way too often.

When I'm done with Weston's hair you can see his ears and most of his forehead. If he wore a suit you'd think he belonged in one. Except for the beard, but it's not a heavy beard. It's the one thing on him he's always kept regularly trimmed. Even my father says Weston has a nice beard as far as beards go.

"You look nice," I tell him.

Weston shakes his head. "Naked," he says.

I brush hair off his shoulder and kiss his neck. I play with his ear. I wet my pinky and poke it in his ear and twist. I want to show him there's no hard feelings, it's just sometimes he pushes me too far.

Weston's still staring in the mirror. He's carried it out with him from the bathroom. He looks me straight in the face and says, "You know, Karla, sometimes you're a real bitch."

We're talking again by the time we get to the lake.

"This is silly," Weston says. He's got his clothes off, heaped under a willow tree: baggy Levis he won't let me wash anymore because if I do they'll disintegrate, t-shirt with a hole in each pit, a sweater with a leather patch on one elbow, a tan spring jacket, pro-Keds, socks, and grey J.C. Penney underwear. We have hard water and even with bleach the whites stay dingy.

"I feel cold already," Weston says. He looks tiny with his hair short and his clothes off.

"Don't be a baby." Sometimes when he whines about this or that I let him, I really do baby him. But today I give him a look that would cream corn.

I've been smoothing out the blanket while Weston's been undressing. Now I undress, folding my clothes carefully and putting them on a corner of the blanket, neatly piled. Weston says I should be more of a free spirit; he says I'm too bound in by order and propriety. Ed's done that to me, he says. He says Ed's kept me from having any kind of imagination.

"Look at your clothes," he says. "I'd expect to see price tags on them, they're all folded up like in the window at Shockheimer's."

Here I am, naked on a March afternoon, and Weston's telling me I'm a prude. He talks like this just to remind himself he's a bohemian, and I'd mind less if it weren't so often at my expense.

"This is as naked as we get," Weston announces. He edges over to the bank and dabs his toes in the water. "Brrr," he says. "I'm not going in unless I'm pushed."

"If I have to," I say. I take a few steps and cannonball off the bank.

Lake Poygan greets my bottom like a slap from a hairbrush. Darts of ice go up the sides of my ribcage and up the crease of my behind. My shoulders feel pinched by it; the top of my head feels crowned. It's maybe four and a half feet deep here, so I settle to the bottom. My toes touch and I crab along, still in a ball. It's good to feel close in on myself. I'm strangely thrilled. I'm going to float to the top in a second but for the life of me I don't want to get out of this ball shape I'm in. I blow out air to keep me on the bottom. I expect to see air bubbles crystallize into ice cubes and go bobbing to the surface, but I don't know if that happened or not because I don't want to open my eyes. I don't want to for the same reason I don't want to get untucked: with my eyes closed and my body curled up on the bottom of Lake Poygan I'm happy.

But finally my air is gone and before I stand up I open my eyes. I don't see anything but the brown-black water and the whiteness of myself. I stand up and feel my breasts shrivel. My stomach pulls up inside me like a hazel nut.

"How is it?" Weston asks me. He's still on shore and he's sucking on his pipe.

"It's fine," I tell him. "Chilly at first, but then it's fine." I throw my hair back and it slaps my shoulders. I'm surprised ice doesn't clatter off the ends.

"Your nipples are all goose-bumped," he says.

"I didn't say it wasn't cold. I said you'll get used to it." I fall on my back and start doing the backstroke to prove it to him. Weston's sitting down and he's laughing.

"Hell of a sight," he shouts.

I stop and tread water.

"Do the backstroke some more," Weston says. "I want to watch."

"Aren't you coming in?"

"No, but bring that chilled behind back here and I'll warm it for you." He puffs on his pipe.

"Are you coming in or not?" I ask.

"This would be a swell scene for my movie," he says. He holds his arms at full length in front of him, making a box with his fingers touching and his thumbs upraised to frame me. "Woman swimming nude, cold spring day, erotic goose-bumped flesh surfaces. Voluptuous breasts. Brazen, wanton face. Her lover waits while she disports herself. Then she returns to him, he towels her off, and they hump with abandon until her cries of ecstasy rend the air."

I don't say anything at first. I can't. It's one of those times when something you've always lived with and more or less accepted suddenly gets to be too much, and all at once I'm shaking and I can barely contain it. If there were anything to throw, and if I could trust my aim, and if I could grip anything in the first place, I'd plant a rock between his eyes.

But then I think of something else. An idea comes to me clearly, as if I've rubbed my eyes after a long sleep and the world is different.

I swim closer, back to where I can stand. I want to cross my arms over my breasts, because it's cold in the willow's shade, but I want Weston to get ideas, so I leave my arms at my sides. "You wouldn't get in the water if your life depended on it," I tell him.

"And it doesn't," he says.

"Your sex life does," I say, convinced I mean this, but Weston's face shows he doesn't believe me. He stands and puts his hands on his hips. "Very funny," he says, holding his hand out for me to take it.

"I'm serious," I say. "You may as well tie a rubber band around your thing and let it turn blue and fall off."

He just glares at me. He can tell I'm serious now.

"Oh, all right." He takes a few steps back and leaps. His splash is tremendous and I get soaked again. He surfaces immediately. "Jesus Christ!" he shouts. He stands with his hands cupped over his crotch. "Satisfied?"

"Not until we race underwater."

"Karla, don't be ridiculous," Weston says.

"Afraid of a little water?" I say.

"I'll lose my medal." He picks the lion off his chest and gives it a shake.

"Toss it on the blanket. One race and then we get dry." I smile. I put on my wanton and hungry look, the one he thinks will be so good in his movie.

"You're a strange woman," he says. But he leaves the necklace on shore and splashes back. We hug. "MMMMM," he says. "Let's skip the race."

"Later, Weston. You'd think the whole world revolved around your pecker." I grab him there and give him a twist until he says, "Ouch!" But I don't let go. I look at Weston hard, our eyes almost level, and I say, "Don't ever forget, Weston, that this little thing in my hand is your only claim to power."

"Oh, I know," he says, a little shocked and anxious.

And then I smile and let go. Weston grins. He thinks everything is better now.

"Winner gets top?" he asks.

"Winner gets top," I say. "But don't be too proud of your California heritage. You smoke too much and your wind's down." Weston knows I can hold my breath for over a minute. I'm counting on his pride and his desire for the thrill of victory. "On three," I say. I'm poised, ready to leap.

"I'll wipe your ass here and on the blanket, too," he says.

I count. "One, two—"

Weston dives. He never waits for three. I watch his toes disappear and then I move.

I don't have time to get dressed, but I figure I can get back to our house with no one seeing me. And if they do, who cares? It's hard to work, though, because my feet aren't steady and I have to look at what my hands are doing. I fumble getting Weston's keys out of his pockets. I have to force my hands to pick up his clothes and put them in the center of the blanket. I put mine there, too. Then I roll up the blanket. I've put on his necklace and it dances across my chest as I bend over and stand again. I've left out his socks and from the picnic basket I take out the bottle of Old Grand Dad and set that next to the socks. I fold the rolled blanket in half. It's clumsy but I can carry it. For a second I think maybe I'll sit down and wait for him to surface so I can see the look on his face. But waiting like that would be too cruel, and besides, I can easily picture it, just like it was a scene from Weston's movie.

Driving our Impala out to California an hour later, with the sun warm on my left arm and with my two suitcases and my favorite Emmylou Harris records in the backseat, I can picture one more scene. I see it as it would appear in Weston's movie: Weston walking the six miles home, coming up our long drive, drunk, stark naked except for his Interwovens. And my father (because before I left I called him to come for supper) waiting on the front porch, sitting on the wicker chair in his green work shirt and his new white and blue pinstripe Oshkosh B'Gosh overalls, sipping a long-necked bottle of Point Special and looking impatient and huge and ornery....

And Weston tells me I have no imagination.

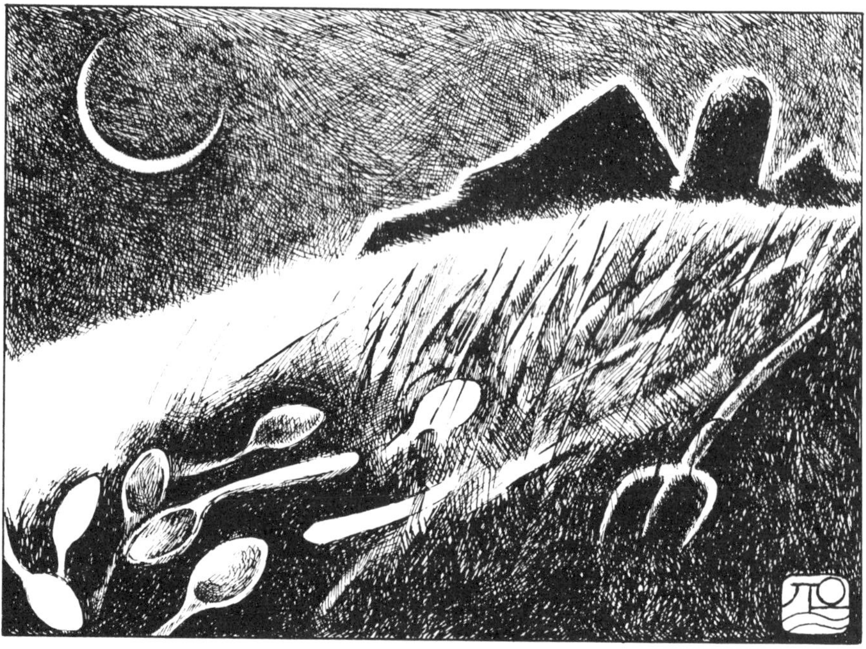

THE NIGHT OF THE SPOON

They're out there, I know. Down by the river, past the willow thicket on that smooth stretch of grass that looks like a green beach. Dancing, music going, probably got their clothes off. Doesn't matter who's married to who with them. They're city folk on a holiday. "Oh, let's be rural," they all laugh and get financing quicker than I ever could and buy up little heaps of earth to put cracker box houses on and think, Now isn't this just the life?

It isn't just the life. It's hardly life at all. I'm reminded every day plowing these fields that should have been done two weeks ago. I'm on the south side of Mosquito Hill, plowing in the dark next to the cemetery my wife's buried in. My delinquent son Norbert, if he's not over there with them, is strolling through the house ceiling-eyed as if he were a fish observing the water's surface, trying to keep a greasy sweep of hair from falling across his face.

I say he's touched. If it were up to me his hair'd be nubbins. I told the people at the correctional home to do that for me, but they refuse to shave Norbert's head down to the bewildered tips of hair I want.

Corn should've been in a week ago, I should already be hearing the seeds crack open in the earth, but it's been wet and the three wheeler doesn't manage well on slippery hills, the close-set front wheels spin and threaten to tumble sideways, so I'm careful. Break your hip once from a spill like that and you learn. Can't look around much, not that I have time or there's much to see in the dark, but I know what's there and somedays it's reassuring to know what you got: to the left my house and then the hill drops away and away into the damned subdivision and then to the river, which is where they party. Not to my right for sure. Across the box-wire fencing saggy with wild blackberry and puffball vines a gravel lane curves over a rise and nudges right past the family plot marked with double stones for my parents and a double stone half-used for Marion and myself. There's also Norbert's brother.

But don't talk to me about his brother. Norbert was a hellion from the word go, always with that smile you couldn't ever trust, but his brother, what his brother did would've made you ache whole. I'm not talking about that time with the tractor—hell, anybody on a good grade, me, 's gonna flip a three-wheeler—

I'm talking about the planned stupidities.

"Luther," his brother says to me, "Luther, I need $10 for the dance."

"What dance?" I say.

"Sadie Hawkins Day Dance," he says.

"Who'd take you?" I say.

"Nobody," he says. "I want the $10 to get pissed on and go bust it up."

"Go on," I say and cuff the side of his head a good one.

So he steals the money from my wallet anyway and Clayton calls me and says he's got him down to the police station and would I come by and take him home? Fifteen and he punched Arnie Otis, one of the parents, right in the stomach for telling him to watch his mouth.

Had Norbert beat hollow. Norbert was just goofy. Had that swoop of hair in his eyes, hell, you pull a lock down straight and he coulda chewed it, so that swoop was always falling down obscuring the world and so what does he do? Does he cut it? No, sir, he tilts his head and walks under his hair trying to get that swoop to fall back over an ear and he ends up with a tick from tilting for that damn swoop. Got his head cocked like his neck's boneless.

It was different when their Ma was alive. She had better rein on both of them. She could theaten them with me, which was better than me threatening them directly. They had all day to think about me wrapping that belt around my hand and that was the same as the fear of God. Later, me hauling off on one or the other carried no weight, it was too quick. The blow came and went and they never had to think about it. Marion had them thinking. The yank on the ear that pulled their heads a quarterturn'd come and then she'd deliver a thunderous, "Wait'll your Pa gets home!" On my own I couldn't ever learn them that respect. Their bad habits took root like horseradish. I caught them once behind the tool barn smoking cigarettes and taking tiny swigs off one of my whiskey bottles. So I say to them, You wanna drink, huh? You wanna smoke, do you? And they scuffle their feet and say, No sir, but they've got these shit-eating grins on their faces like what does he know so I says to them, I say, All right, smoke up then. And I mash a cigarette in each face and say, Light that and of course they can't the cigarette's busted so I make them take new ones and light them and I tell them to puff it down, puff it down, goddamnit! And then I make them smoke another right away and another right after that and so on and so on until they're both getting red in the face and green and coughing raw like pneumonia settled in them and I keep making them smoke one cigarette after the other until they've each gone through a pack and they've sunk to their knees now, their rib cages shaking, eyes watering, mouths hanging drool and I say, Have a slug of that whiskey now, boys. And Norbert's brother says to me, Please, Pa, don't. And I slap him one and say, Don't please pa me you son of a bitch and I hand Norbert the bottle and say take a good slug of that and Norbert tips the bottle just barely to his lips and I say, Whoa, now, not that little and I tip it way back on him till it streams over his face and his eyes get wide with fear and hope and he knows he won't ever come up for air again until he glugs it down till I say stop and finally he does that and then it's the same with his brother and when their stomachs turn the flip flops and begin boiling up their throats I say to them, Remember, boys, this is the way things turn out and I walk away with the bottle and they're left keeled over, puke flying from their wracked-out stomachs.

It didn't do any good, of course. It got to be a game with them. How much of the old man's whiskey can you swallow before you get sick? Can we get a bottle out and get Katie Plamann pissed enough she'll do it for us? Bastards both, but Norbert's brother was the real one. He got goofy Norbert to do everything—let the air out of Clayton's tires, tape the nozzles down on scented hair spray or room deodorizer and toss the fuming bomb into somebody's car, then roll up the windows, bust windows at the widow Harriet's (she wasn't a widow, she was an old maid, but she was engaged once, during the war, so we gave her the benefit of the doubt), filch cigarettes from Sefert's, piss like dogs on the mourners' cars parked in front of the Borchart Funeral Home, tear around town at night, horns going, tossing empties onto the street to smash or clatter like the hoofbeats of runaway horses. And Norbert usually got caught, not his brother. Norbert was always just slow enough, clumsy enough, to be the one to fall over the fence, land in a heap, trip over himself getting up and wind up collared by whomever's trash heap they'd set fire to. His brother was gone, clean as a ghost.

Problems on all sides and I'm talking about Norbert and his brother.

It's the goddamned subdivision. Nelson's got to go and sell the land to Porter Atwood without so much as talking to me to see if I wanted it. Porter, that son of a bitch. Porter's got Milo's place across the road already and now Nelson's. Milo's he lets sit there untouched just so it hangs over me. Nelson's, though, he smells green money with Nelson's. What're there now, seven, eight houses already? You turn around to sneeze and another one's been thrown together and stapled shut. I checked one out the last Sunday. Half-inch plywood and hope. Joists held together with sheet staples. One car garages bigger than the living rooms and bedrooms combined. Not a straight line anywhere—gaps filled with wood putty or a snatch of insulation. The roof went on without a pitch base or even tar paper—just shingles nailed over the plywood. I've done cattle sheds with corrugated tin and capped nails that are more water dry. But he fills them and fills them, and the people poured in all scoot through my land, my woods down by the river, as if it were God's own acre.

Now Porter wants the river property. He says he'll take it off my hands at 750 an acre if I toss in a 60′ width of land running from the road back there so he has access to it. Otherwise, he can only offer me 500.

"Porter," I tell him, "since when you think I'm so stupid I'll give you land so you can build a road I'll pay the taxes on?"

"Come now," Porter says. "Town board wouldn't do that. I'd fix it up with Matty Keillor."

"She's not your fool, Porter. One or two go-rounds with you don't make her beholden to you. And I ain't either. You think about 2500 a square foot and till you can do that without gulping, don't come back bothering me when I've chores to do."

"Luther," Porter says, "Luther, you're being ridiculous. I believe you're holding against me for something twenty years ago, Luther. You were the one that married her. Ain't that enough to speak well of me? I backed off. She got sweet on you and I backed off, didn't I? We've been down the road a ways since then, Luther. I helped bury your son, didn't I? Didn't I feel grief deep as yours? It was like I buried one of my own, Luther. I cried for the waste of it, the terrible waste."

"I know what you sell those houses for, Porter."

Now the earnest grief thrown over his face from a second ago is gone and his mouth is working in a wink and a grin, like we're buddies sharing the same tired joke. "A man's got to live. Get what you can get, right?"

"Not from me, Porter. You're not getting anything from me."

Porter throws his arms wide as if he wanted to hug, to take in all the earth, far as you can see. "It's a dream of theirs, Luther—their own home! I can give them that dream. I can do it, but I need your cooperation. You wanna take all those people's dreams away?" Porter's eyes get all soggy like he actually believes the shit he's peddling. I can see why he's had the women he's had. Ben Keillor's widow, Suzie Johnson, some say the widow Harriet, I don't know how his wife puts up with it. He even had Marion, and so many since her it's like Marion didn't matter, she's just a little mark on his calendar from some long gone year. He keeps the calendars in his safe along with the deeds from all the farms he's collected—farms he orginally sold one time and is gathering back because enough people want them now it won't do to keep them farms, not when you can slice them into swatches and put a cracker-box house on each one and sell each half-acre for 10,000 and the house for 50 and the people think they're getting some kind of deal. He keeps cutting the swatches smaller and smaller and as more people come the price swells and swells and with the new money he buys up more farms. It's a good business, I can't fault him for doing right by himself, for sure—nobody else around here could've done what he did so quickly. Nobody else would've wanted to, though, either. Or they'd have wanted to but didn't have his gumption. That's what it is really, ruthless gumption pretending innocence.

I just can't square with myself how he remembers that time with Marion like she was a co-op and when I ended up with majority shares I got her. And for getting the better of him on that deal, I'm supposed to owe him something now. He's got his eyes on my place, too—the whole place, not just the back acreage or the access road. He wants mine for a ski hill—not something major, but enough. He'd make it a resort and get steady money—not the single plunk! of money on his counting table but plunk! after plunk! after plunk! He can just barely keep the drool off his chin when he stands on the hilltop by my shed and looks down and across. Tow ropes out there, a lodge up here, groomed trails, ice rinks and sled runs, a water slide and go-cart track for summer, a restaurant. Yes, sir, Porter the entrepenuer. Porter the son of a bitch.

The people he sells those houses to never stay either. Starter homes is what they are, a first house for couples with a baby or thinking about one, and once the baby's there or the second one they realize how really tiny the place is, the sink you can't get both elbows into, the refrigerator door you have to move the table to open, the bathroom you can't shit in and shave two people together. So they jack up the price 8 thou and move on and the next people think How lovely! There's a woods right down there for the kid to play in and I'll bet it's good for grouse, too, and whitetail. And never mind it's posted, he doesn't really mean that, after all, we're neighbors now, right?

Neighbors: mine is mine and yours is mine. That's neighbors.

They're younger, too. This last batch, they're not even married. Doesn't matter to Porter. Sign here, please, what you say your names were, Hedgetoff and Macy? Not into combining, huh? Nah, don't worry, I'm a liberal man. So's your neighbor—Luther Krake. Big and surly, but don't you mind. His woods're a great place to picnic. Yeah, by the river. Quite a little party spot, know what I mean? Party for two, eh? I know how it is when you're young. Stretched out a few times myself—don't tell my missus—Hah!—she thinks I'm done stretching.

So Porter's got what used to be Nelson's lower corn field full up with eight houses with eight couples, married or not, with their bastard kids firing BB's into my herd like they were dropping pigeons off the phone wires. I've found BB's lodged in bloody eyes, imbedded in teats. They're Norbert's kind of people. His brother's too. Smart-mouthed and fast about it, life turning somersaults for them because they're not old yet and they work in Appleton where work is getting paid for picking your belly-button on the swing shift. At night the barbecue fires flare and the music cranks up. Guitar noise and a thum-thumping so incessant I got to call over there three times a night to tell them to shut up, my cows got to sleep even if I don't. The phone call balms them for a half-hour tops. Then zoom! the music screams into the night again and I hear their screeches as one after another of them goes skinny-dipping in the river.

I could tolerate it before they all knew each other. Norbert and his brother went around last summer introducing themselves, looking for free beers and it ended up quite a party. I heard a lot of laughter and the clinking of beer bottles echoing from the sheds—my sheds, away from their places, and I found Norbert and his brother back there with two or three men and four or five women. They were all laughing and grouped so you couldn't tell who belonged to who. The men were in sport shirts with the tails hanging out and the women wore those halter things, their arms purply white under the bug lights. Norbert and his brother were giving a lecture on how to piss into long-necked empties. They'd set a row of four empties against the shed and each man was lined up across from one, their peckers out and Norbert's brother explaining how the one who got the most in his bottle gets to choose the girl he wanted, marriage rings or no, the next most-filled bottle the next woman and so on. The women giggled and the men guffawed, but what they didn't know was Norbert's brother was serious. He'd win the pissing gamble and take the hand of whatever woman'd eyed him enough while they were getting drunk enough to piss in bottles and off he'd go with her down to the river before her husband or whoever'd figured he was doing just what he'd said.

So the women commented on what they saw and Norbert raised his hand and dropped it and his brother said, Stand back! Stand back, y'all, I need the arc, as if he were a Southern cracker and that broke up everyone so the two other men started pissing on their pant legs and Norbert wrote names on the wall in piss while his brother let fly with a lemon-colored stream that hissed and arced and fell splashing on the shed wall and then fell plumb into the bottle with a thundering like horses dancing in one place and then he walked to the bottle as the arc flattened and he finished by standing right over the bottle shaking the last few drops off so they fell into the bottle like he was dropping coins.

"Overlarge *and* accurate," he said, holding the bottle up like he'd just produced the cure for cancer. "Now," he said, his pecker still hanging out, "which of you lovely ladies want to go for a moonlight ride without the horse?" The men sort of laughed then but their wives or whatever didn't. He stood in front of each one and did a deep kneebend and straightened up and both the first woman and the second looked down and then away as if she'd seen what she thought she'd seen and didn't want to look anymore but the third woman, a woman with skinny arms and corrugated blonde hair that swung down her back reached out with her index finger and then tapped the end of it as if to say, There, that's it, and her husband or whatever said, "Now just a second, Jeannie—" and took a step forward and Norbert's brother squared to face him, he was bigger than the husband and his rising penis looked like some kind of weapon and the husband froze and sort of whined, "Jeannie—" and Norbert's brother laughed, he hadn't even had to hit the man and I was going to step in then, they didn't know I was there, out of the light, and say, "Enough!" but when you got right down to it, I thought, why bother?

Since then it's been a them versus us kind of thing. It's been that way for me since day one, since the foundations were laid over there—poured cement on sand, no basements, but after that night they've felt the same. Dead cats get thrown on my steps, pumpkins get thrown at the mailbox from speeding cars, leaving a mess of orange pulp and twisted metal. They poured paint remover on my car one night, when I drive past they look up from their flower beds or the compost heaps they're tending to smile or laugh at the car that's molting. Even after Norbert's brother went in the river and Norbert started hanging out with them again, it's been them versus us. But Norbert's one of them, walking out from under his hair and locating his mouth with a beer bottle pointer while his ears close up to anything decent.

The one called Jeannie was at the funeral. She cried twice. In front of the casket and when they were carrying him out. Her skinny body shook under the white satiny top she wore and she sniffled to herself. I couldn't figure it. It'd been months since that contest by the sheds and everybody knew about him and Cindi Kucksdorff. I couldn't see why this Jeannie was carrying on. I'd thought she'd be ashamed to weep for someone like that. If it'd been up to me I'd of left them in the river. An accident, the coroner said. Accidental drowning. High alcohol content. Two a.m., late September. A woman and her companion, both intoxicated, drowned after the woman's companion lost control of the car and drove off the Stephensville bridge (a bridge since widened) into twelve feet of water, the car coming to rest on its side in heavy silt. The couple became tangled, disoriented, and died before they could free themselves.

Not included in the coroner's report, but public knowledge anyway: Cindi Kucksdorff was found with her mouth in Norbert's brother's lap, his pants undone, his child in her belly. And what I know and Norbert knows and maybe Cindi but nobody else: he had his Great Lakes traveling papers and would've been in Sinapore or someplace before she started to show. Accident? They should have been left in the river, left in that tipped-sideways car with the white bass and redhorse staring at them through the windshield.

Except for the contours getting tricky, I like plowing in the dark. When the boys were young and Marion was still alive I took them for rides that way, from late afternoon till past dusk right up till their bedtime. We were engulfed by engine noise and dark, yellow cones of light thrown out in front. I'd furrow around the young corn till midnight, but around 8:30 Marion'd come and scoop them off to bed, one on each hip. But until she came I'd have one boy on each side, each one gripping the fender as they sighted down opposite sides of the tractor watching the crumpled earth being eaten by my machine. Then Marion carried them off to bed and I would think how one day with enough of a loan there'd be three of us on tractors in a staggered row. Plowing, discing, dragging, seeding, cutting, harvesting, and plowing again. Come hay time one driving the baler, one the rake, and one on the wagon stacking. Me and Norbert and Norbert's brother Dana, because when he was still that young he had that name, Dana, and hadn't become Norbert's brother.

He became Norbert's brother because I realized how good a chance there was he wasn't my son.

It went like this: Marion was seeing Porter and me, only she'd been seeing Porter off and on since high school and me only since that January, when I was twenty. We were both sweet on her because she was a big-boned girl and solid, with heavy ankles and legs used to work. German stock—a wide, flat face but pretty. So she alternated seeing us, never telling us about the other though how could you not know and I, at least, kept pestering her about him. One night I'm working my hands inside her blouse but daren't yet go for the fasteners behind when she says to me, "If we do, will you never ask me about Porter Atwood again? Not ever?" and I said, Oh, yes, not ever, and her body, arms and chest and back, went from rigid to slack and her blouse got opened and her skirt got pulled up and for about fifteen minutes in her father's '53 Ford sedan we sweated into each other, all frantic and afraid to make noise and then it was over and I asked her to marry me. And Dana was born (premature, everyone said) and two years later Norbert was and never once did I ask Marion about Porter and I wasn't going to, either, because that was before me, even when it was him and me for that spell there it seemed like that was before me, I mean really before.

One day when Dana was nearly ten I took him into town to pick up some 40-30-30 for the corn and afterwards we stopped at Leeman's Cafe for coffee and a sweet roll and milk for Dana and there's Porter plumped down at the counter, round-shouldered over an egg breakfast.

"'Mornin', Porter," I say and he says, "'Morning', Luther," and chases some egg around his plate. Dana and I go sit in a booth.

Pretty soon Porter gets another cup of coffee and joins us. Doesn't sit down, just stands there, holding the cup at half-mast on his belly. Looking Dana and me up and down real good.

"That's liable to be your boy, ain't it?" he asks.

I say, "Yep, this here's my #1 hired hand. You've seen him in town before, haven't you, Porter?"

"Oh, yes, but not since he's grown some. Big enough for me to get a look at him. Marion's first, right? I was wonderin' how he turned out. He looks good." He touches Dana on the shoulder, gives him a shake. "You look good, son. Real fine." He grins at both of us like he knows something.

You can get to some crazy thinking all day on a tractor. Thinking too much or not at all. And that night spreading fertilizer on the green new shoots I got to thinking how Marion was when we were married and how just before that—it was before, wasn't it?—she'd been seeing Porter and me both, though what seeing meant I didn't know and was too afraid to ask, too afraid after I'd pushed and pushed and Marion'd shushed me up forever with her body and I was so grateful for that I recollected events differently until Porter that day made his backhanded claim and so finally that night I did ask because I needed to know if it'd been me she'd been full of twice and she laughed as if thinking of something very amusing and said, "Oh, come now, Luther, what do you think?" And my tongue caught in my throat and I shook my head as if I'd disremembered what it was I was thinking and I was thinking how Marion was too smart for me, playing things close to her chest like that and right there I realized Norbert's brother was not my child, he couldn't be, and all the next day I brooded on that and that next night when Marion came for the children I told her, no, Norbert's brother was older and he was going to stay with me a spell, because rank has its privileges, after all, and I'd bring him in later.

At the far end of the field, by the fence line that divides this lower field from the river plot, the headlights caught a gleam of silver and I said to the boy, go see what that is now and he hopped from his seat on the fender and appeared all yellow in the headlights, bending to see what had flashed silver. The tractor idled, rumbling, snuffling, as if constantly clearing its throat. It happened then. I had this one moment of clear vision, the tractor slipping back in gear, the gigantic rear wheel spinning forward, the boy crushed into the field, and I would have the grief of the accident but nothing else, no more doubts, but the boy turned, smiled, held up an overlarge soup spoon clodded with dirt, and he forever became Norbert's brother and lived.

Marion took pneumonia that winter, when Norbert was nine, his brother eleven, and after a month of not getting out of bed she died. Sometimes I think she willed herself to stay there after I turned from her, reluctantly but turned, and she let what was in her eat her up. That's another of my doubts: that she didn't much want to live after what I believed I knew but didn't know really ruined us both.

Norbert came home yesterday from the county detention facility. He takes one more car without asking its owner's permission, especially if like the last time he busts it up in the chase that follows, he's going to Oshkosh to do some real time in the real place. But Norbert's too goofy to think that, he just keeps walking out from under his hair as if the one thing he's got going for himself is that haircut.

He's over there now. A burst of laughter cuts through the tractor's cough and I idle it down, listening. It's dark now, truly dark, and through the trees the river flashes black and silver. Bodies are moving down there, there's a splash and then another. They've set up one of those boxes on a tree stump and they've got the air shuddering while they dance. Pale bodies. Norbert dancing with his head cocked on his shoulder. In the water and out. Laughter. Pagan rites, right in my own backyard. A mile from where his brother leaped the guardrail. The river smells of death each spring and they're dancing in it.

There's something in me that's been there since I thought I knew about his brother and wanted vengeance. Or maybe I've had it always. One time I visited a cousin in Milwaukee whose son lived on the eleventh floor of a downtown highrise, cars zipping past on the interstate directly beneath. His son laughed and said sometimes when he got home from work he'd look at the cars through his binoculars and approached understanding, how if he had a scope and rifle, not the binoculars, he'd be tempted to shoot. Like dropping rocks on ants, he said, and his wife said, That's terrible! and we men laughed, of course, because we were nervous, because he'd said what we all felt.

I feel that now. I want to chase them down with the tractor, unhook the plow in this spot and scatter them all, the big wheels churning clods of earth in a sprayed wake behind me. I want to show them what this life is all about. I think about the gun strapped under the tractor seat, a shotgun loaded with shot and the extra shells, shot and slung and rocksalt, in the toolbox. Just a few shots above their heads, I think. A few shots into the trees shattering branches, the flat whine of bullets boring into the moon. But it would be too great, the pull too great to sight down the ribbed blue barrel and feel the clean straight line of connection between my eye and the bullet and that pale body shaking off water by the river's edge.

The tractor rumbles through my body. It's constant, the rumbling, but I go days not noticing it. Just as I don't look to the right when I'm near the cemetery fence. It's something you get used to, something that's there always, but you act like it's not. Funny how you can ignore something like that. Funny, too, how I invent what she would say to me. She scolds me when I'm angry. "Luther, they're children dancing," she says. She's wrong but I believe her, believe her long enough for the heat to ebb. I want to argue. "To whom do I leave this place?" I ask. "Who? Porter's going to get it—either for a percentage of the loans on it, the unpaid mortgage, or because Norbert'll sell it for the price of a mobile home and gas money to Florida."

"Leave it to Norbert anyway," she says and when I say Why? she says, "Because he's our child, Luther, and what else do you have to give him?"

That night of the spoon comes back to me, the night I handed my life over to doubt. She knows, of course. Nothing was ever said in the time that followed but she knows. I answer to her for everything I do.

"Let them dance," I say, pulling the throttle down hard, pulling it low so the tractor leaps forward as if it were alive, so the tombstones rip past and glow like shimmering teeth. "Let them all dance."

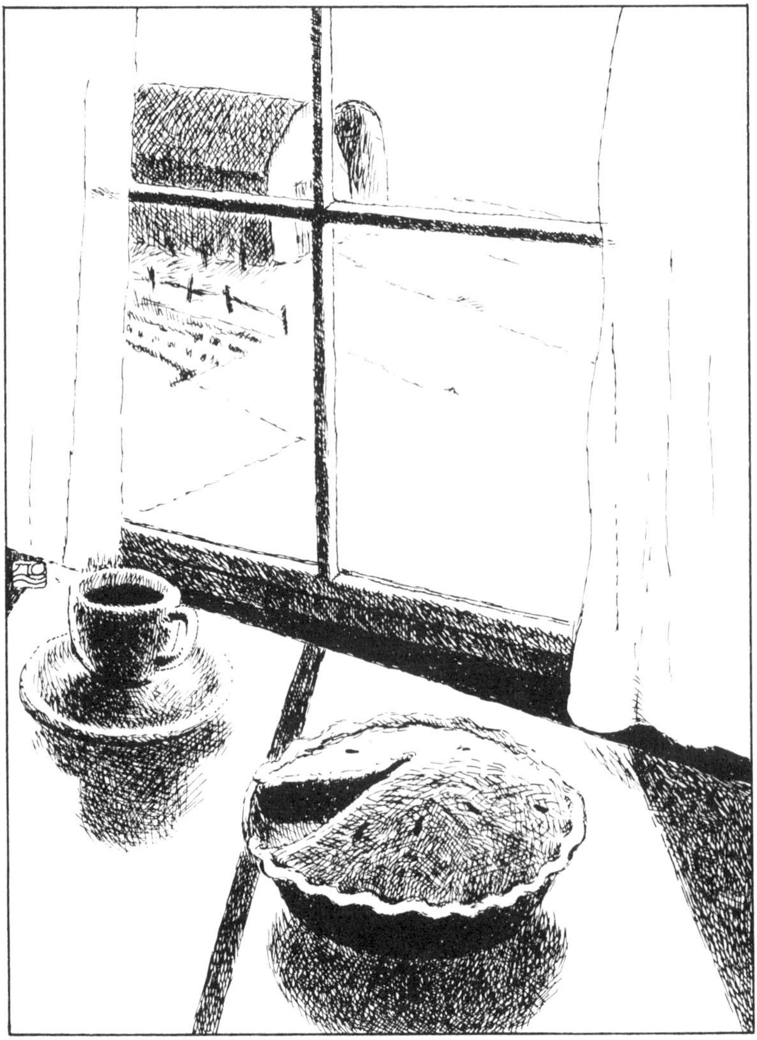

KITCHENS

Herb Tessen's kept after me. He's caught me at a weak, unthinking moment and now I'm with him at a church dinner where everyone's looking for companionship to die with. It's been four years since that Cecil Alt business, when I was hostage in the town hall to Cecil and his shotgun, after which I stepped blind into the afternoon sun and there was Herbert, hands in his pockets, looking like he'd been impatiently waiting for me to finish shopping. I tried to ignore him, even when he took my arms and shook me and said, "Matty, are you all right?" and I said yes I'm fine and drove home, not even sure how I got out of his grip or if he walked me to my car or not and I had a cup of tea with brandy to get back to focusing on things.

And in the time since then, Herbert surprisingly kept calling me up for breakfasts I refuse, and then he drops in to eat his lunch at my desk, his mouth going like some rachety old machine, crumbs grinding out the corners of his mouth, while he asks me the same questions every day as if their repetition would encourage me to change my answers: how you doing—fine—nice day—yes—thought about marrying me—no—well, see you tomorrow.

Then he didn't come for a month and I almost got to missing him, especially since Leona commented on it so much, and then he asked me to this dinner, didn't say anything through two full sandwiches and then just sprung it and without even thinking I said, all right, and as soon as he was gone, his Hi yoo! bellowing from the street, I looked at Leona's face and realized I'd done the wrong thing.

Redeemer Lutheran Church has the same people for their monthly Spares and Pairs Dinner as get together for cards and bingo Thursday nights at St. Stephen's Catholic Church down the street. Every so often someone does ask someone to get married and everyone feels good about it, as if they've each had a hand in its happening, and this is what Herbert wants for us, as if magic will descend on me and I'll give up my papal claptrap and become Lutheran, but more importantly, I'll press his shirts, soak hair grease off his collars, cook up T-bone dinners, occasionally perform the other thing, and have eggs ready at 6am, with toast burned beyond recognition, little flecks of black dust propelled across the table by a stray breeze.

I sit, hands folded in my lap, while he introduces me too loud, deep white lines appearing in his face as he says my name—"Matty Keillor!"—as if I were being auctioned off to each of them. "Matty Keillor, my girl!"

I nod as if I'm meeting these people for the first time. They're looking at Herb and me with a knowledge I know is wrong. Whatever Herbert's told you is a mistake, we're not what you think we are. I started smoking cigarettes after Ben died, and now I yearn for a smoke as if I can draw life through a straw. I've not said boo! since dinner started, Herb's talked and I've nodded or shaken my head and for him this is the same as conversation.

Now they're clearing dishes and Herb's lit his pipe, cheeks billowing, the stubble on his chins standing straight out like soldiers. Soon the Women's Guild members will roll up the table-cloths and the bingo cage will be trundled out, cards dispersed, and Reverend Bill Hollington will call out the first number and they'll serve coffee and pretzels (the Catholics have beer and popcorn).

Finally I say to Marge Peterson across from me, "Excuse me for a cigarette" and start to get up, but Herb grabs my bony wrist and says, "Hold on, Mattie, it's okay to smoke right here. See this?" He holds up his pipe which he's been tamping and lighting since the chicken bone plates were cleared, but I shake my head, and shrugging his shoulders and grinning as if to say, "An independent woman," he lets me go.

I lean against Tony Trauber's front fender and shake out a cigarette. I fumble getting it straight in my mouth. I hate the things really, but after Ben and Rupert I felt my life should change in some way, even if it hadn't.

It's then I see Luther working the cedar hedge that runs alongside the church garage. The muscles in his arms are so large they're flat, their only definition comes from the pressure he exerts on the long arms of the shears and then the muscles rise slowly, as if two continents, one in his biceps, the other his forearms, had woken and shrugged off sleep. Legs like a dock worker's, low as if he were about to sit down. All trunk like a great elm, his oval head salt and peppered with a greying crewcut. A tight little paunch, his chest settling like his legs. Power. In a way he reminds me of myself—pretty much lean, bandy-legged, sort of sewn together from muscle and coarse thread. A branch from the hedge falls sideways, tipped like one of those English guards fainting in place. Luther pulls it out, tosses it on the pile.

"Tithing, Luther?" Everyone knows why he works at the church, but he explains when anyone asks.

"Reverend's arrangement with Marion. She's got me near the church if not in it."

"You could always not."

"No," he says, "since she died it's been too much a habit."

I nod. "You should be downstairs. Card games'll start once the women get tired of bingo."

"I'm not much for cards."

We're talking as he works from the hedge to the pile and back again. He cuts the hedge with a motion I remember from every spring since I was a little girl, the shears opening and closing like a seed driller for hand-planting corn. I had to fight my brothers for my turn. Later, I fought my children for them to take theirs. Except for Fred, reluctant farmers all. Luther pulls another branch loose, leaves it in the driveway. Another and then another, in a line, not stacking them by the garage door. His way of ending the conversation.

Herbert from behind us, "Looks like you got yourself an audience, Luther." He stands next to me and taps his pipe into the ashtray I'm holding. His fingers are littered with charred bits of tobacco. "People wondering where you got off to, Matty. I said I'd fetch you. The ladies are doing dishes. Ain't that right, Luther? We don't have 'em doing the dishes while the cards get dealt, they'd lose all our money before we'd have a chance to."

Luther wipes a trickle of sweat that's running down beside his ear, another under his nose. I dump the ashtray over an open garbage can. "I was telling Luther about the Street Dance," I say. "I was saying he should come, he gets into town so little." Luther turns his head and I feel understanding arc between us.

Herb escorts me downstairs. "Luther never goes to the Street Dance," as if that settles something.

I wash dishes and hand them to Marge Peterson, who rinses them and hands them to Robert Engstrom, her twenty-nine-year-old date. Marge is forty-ish, a blimp. I mean, I'm not pretty, but at least my wrinkles stay close to the bone. Robert's an elongated pink man with whitewalls curving over his waxen, stuck-out ears. He always wears black suits to match his hair and white shirts and tiny, polka-dotted ties. He's in insurance and while he towel dries dishes he looks at the men who aren't as if he's suddenly aware there are lions and there are ostriches and he can't figure out how he got transformed into an ostrich. A man belches. Katie Pearson, pouring sugar back into a gallon jar, says, "Excuse yourself, John" and John Pearson grouches an apology.

Everyone here seems somehow crippled.

I wipe the chicken goo and remnant suds off the webbing between my fingers. Herbert's at one of the small card tables, the man next to him dealing euchre.

"I just remembered, Herbert, I promised Fred and Mary I'd babysit little Martha. They're going over to Kimberly for a movie."

"But—"

"I'm sorry, but I promised."

I get my purse from under my chair. Herbert drapes my sweater over my shoulders. I take it off and put my arms through. "Old women wear them draped," I tell him. "I still need the use of my arms, thank you, and I'm not about to stop, even if Fred does the farming now."

I want to go home and thin onions. Stick my fingers into cool earth with the waning sun still warm on my back and pluck things into life.

Luther's tossing branches into the back of his GMC and I'm set to get into my car—Fred's Mustang, he has my Plymouth to do the shopping with, I've inherited his car because of Martha, a family needs a four door—but just as Luther's motor guns to life I find myself running towards his truck, which stops for traffic on Roosevelt.

Luther's face is oval, with black slits for eyes and mouth. There's a mole on his elbow and I talk to that. "I'm serious about the Street Dance."

"Sure you're not just getting back at Herbert?"

"That's part of it."

"I won't ask what's the rest." His face kinder now, the eyes glint but not like steel.

"It's two months away," I say. "How about something before that? We could see if the Street Dance is worth it."

"All right," he says. "I'll call for next week."

"Fair enough," and we shake. He drives off, the truck ka-bumping into the street, and on my way back to the Mustang I remind myself, "You are not a cedar hedge."

Mary's the first one I tell. The only person I'm close enough to talk with. Oh, Fred, but you can't talk with sons the way you do with daughters, even daughters-in-law. She's washing the morning dishes now, I offered to help, but she said no, she doesn't do my dishes when she eats at my house, so I just watch Martha gnaw on her Zweiback.

"Lord, how she eats."

"She likes baby onions, too," Mary says, "but then she futzes funny."

"Fred liked onions, too. He used to have them with his peanut butter."

"Fred will have onions with anything." She glances at the wall clock. "You should've been in the town hall half an hour ago."

"Maybe I just feel like a late start." I pour myself coffee, make a show of sitting down to have it.

"Maybe." Mary wipes her hands on a towel, quick punches as if she were a young boxer. She has an energy to her suited for farm wifery. When I was younger I had it too. Sometimes it still flashes. I throw myself at the garden in a fury that leaves weeds piled to brown and wither, all the rows and the black earth between them so ordered it looks like church. Mary has that energy now, with a wide Irish face that'll hold her prettiness and the bones necessary for taking on the life she has. I know this life. I see the children beyond Martha and count myself lucky to be sixty and past all that.

"So what is it, Matty?"

"Nothing. Foolishness, really. I asked Luther Krake to the Fourth of July Street Dance."

She laughs. "And Herbert's going to sit home alone?"

"This isn't for laughing."

Mary starts mopping down the counter. "Hasn't Herbert already asked you?"

"No."

"So you haven't got a problem, do you?" She giggles. "My mother-in-law's got a date. Hmmm." She laughs, stops when she sees me. "You must admit—"

"I don't admit anything. It's foolishness, like I told you."

She wipes down the table, the crumbs into her palm, and I'm obliged to pick up my cup.

"What'd he say?"

"Who?"

"Luther! Has he said he's going with you?"

"We've a practice date this Thursday."

She pulls up a chair next to me, rests her chin on her knuckles. "What do you think of him?"

"I can't say. I'm not even sure why I asked, except he was there and he wasn't Herbert." She regards me critically. "But I like him," I say, and she allows herself to smile.

He takes me to Taco Bell.

"What's the matter?" he asks me, while swallowing the first half of his third burrito. I don't say anything, just fold my arms together and elbow away the tray.

Luther swallows, then his tongue does a running dance around his mouth, his lips ballooning a section at a time. He tosses back most of his Mountain Dew and runs his tongue again, then wipes his mouth and leaves the napkin balled in his fist.

"I should've taken you somewhere else."

"I think so," I say.

"I wasn't thinking, you know? I mean, I thought the sport shirt was enough."

He must be what? fifty-four and still he rolls up the cuffs on his short-sleeved shirts two inches to show his biceps, only there's no bicep, just a solid mass that tucks in at the elbow and then the forearm starts, wired with black hair and burned brown and red underneath. The V of his shirt is open, but the coloring stops white in a curve just above his collar bone. Take off his shirt and he's fish-belly white in a t-shirt outline. I think of my children tatooed by the sun. Fred's tan a tank-top outline, his arms red as the Ferguson, his shoulders white with flakes. Frankie had a sleeveless tan, wore sportshirts with the sleeves cut off, his neck stayed white, his thorax a branded V. Always his ears peeled fiercely. In winter they were dotted with freckles. Ben's was like Luther's, same generation, Hanes on special or J.C. Penney three packs. Sportshirts for Sunday dinner or church. Ties for funerals and weddings. The last tie Ben wore was for his own funeral. If he'd lived another month he could've worn one to Rupert's.

Stop it.

This man in the brown and orange paisley sport shirt, a style popular fifteen years ago, though that hardly matters, is not Ben, though he dresses like Ben

81

(everyone dresses like Ben), nor is he a replacement for Rupert, dead, or Frankie, gone, gone, gone. Everyone gone somewhere, even Rose.

Let me count my children: no, not either. Luther's into an apology that goes beyond the location of dinner and I'm not listening: "... and since then I've had no mind to manners. Haven't thought at all, Matty, I'm sorry."

What has he said? Since when has he lost manners? Since his son's Dana's death? Marion's? Since Norbert went to Alaska? This man's been talking to me and I've not heard him. How many times does a man really talk to you? Luther's tried earlier than most, confusion and doubt breaking over his face, this opening up letting in a sea that distorts his features, and all I can give in exchange is a simple smile and a suggestion that we go somewhere for coffee. The sea recedes. His face all lines and angles again, slices of leather.

"How about a movie then?"

"Hell, there's nothing I'd want to see."

"There's got to be something." I grab a *Post-Crescent* from the rack in front and thumb to the back of the community news for the movie listings. Nothing he'd like but *Notorious* at the Campus in Appleton.

"We could see that," he says, "only there'll be so many kids."

"Anywhere you go there's kids."

"No, you know. The campus. I mean, two worlds, right?"

"Well, there's always coffee."

"Hell," he says, talking to himself. He looks at me. "You know how often they're in my woods?"

So he drives us over and parks in the faculty lot and we stroll over to the theater on Wisconsin Avenue, only we're not good at strolling. Our pace is off and Luther constantly hitches his stride to accomodate me. Also, he's nervous about his hands and they don't swing normally at his side. They're like birds on a string, rising only to pause, aware they're tethered. Twice he tried to light my cigarette and stops without doing so. The third time we both cup our hands and stand still, then start walking again, me with double steps to align ourselves. I clutch my purse in front of me.

Luther gives me a sidelong look. "The way you walk," he says. "You remind me of Marion."

"I'm not somebody dead," I say.

Luther draws back, genuinely hurt. Good.

"I don't mean don't talk about her. Or even think about her. But I'm not her and I want that clear straight off. She's dead and I'm not and I'm not going to feel sorry about the difference. Do you feel bad about Ben being dead? No."

"I understand."

"You probably don't," I say, "but I'm going to give you the benefit of the doubt, same as I would anyone."

Later I'm in my nightie, one of two pink ones and I'm brushing with less-than-vigorous strokes the thatch of cherry-wood sticks I call my hair. I think about the rest of the evening: how in the movie theater when Ingrid Bergman has so much trouble getting down the stairs it's Luther's hand which seeks out mine in the dark, his calloused pads resting gently on the back of my hand and I find that strangely telling, as if we both wished we were younger. In the kitchen I make myself a cup of tea and the wood floor is cool beneath my feet. I study the tiny blue and red and green riverlines plaited through my calves and ankles and cracked sore feet and think how we said good night without kissing, how Luther backed out of the drive, his head poked over his shoulder with maybe one longing glance into the straw and chaff-strewn bed of his pickup where, and I know this because my look was with longing, too, had we been perhaps forty years younger we'd be rolling and dirtying ourselves, sweating out our passion, parked on some deserted access road only the cows know about.

It's in the morning as I watch Mary, exasperated, hanging out wash behind the mobile home she and Fred have behind my house and constantly plucking Martha back down on her blanket from which she crawls to pluck off petals from the roses or petunias or knock over the laundry basket trying to pull herself to her feet, then tumbles backwards, the sheets rising like clouds over her, that I think about my children.

A litany, then: Matthew, Amanda, Rupert, Frankie, Isabel, Rose and Fred. All married now but Rupert, who'd have wanted a family but died, and Frankie, whom I don't know about except that he has a child and maybe a woman he lives with, and Rose who'll not marry ever, which seems to bother her less as she realizes how many bad marriages there are, which of course means it bothers her more, but who am I to chip in my two cents when she's managing her grief at arm's length?

Besides, whatever the conflict between Rosie's words and her thoughts, she's right, all marriages are bad in one way or another, mostly because people end up with half lives as they try to make one life between them. It's what you create or salvage besides the badness that makes people marry so much—that small hope, shrunken from when you started, that there's still something to create or salvage.

Matthew writes me from Maine, letters he begins and his children finish: "We love you, Grandma. Love Terry." "Mommy says we should write you, so I am. Love Patricia" (a realist, Patricia doesn't believe in writing someone she's never seen), and "la la la, lala, la. Love, Daniel," transcribed and signed by Matthew. The letters finished with a postscript from Kathy, noting the two eldest's progress in school and Daniel's misadventures with a sand crab. And always the double sign-off, as if they write from a well-meaning echo chamber—"we must travel and see you soon—Kathy" "Yes, as soon as the boats allow us. Love, Matt."

Half the words on the page are love, yet at this distance, how can it touch me except as a curiosity? The way Matthew talks, I'm not sure it's something with the boats or with him and Kathy, maybe both. He left here to get away from farming and ended up with tractors on the ocean. "But maybe this Christmas," he assures me. I say all right, and then I get Daniel cooing in my ear and in the background Kathy persuading Patricia to say something to me.

Minor failures of connection. It's harder when the kitchen table, a weary white, is all that separates you in physical distance. A shrug won't do. There's this other person, Amanda, and you wonder how she could have possibly come from your flesh.

Badness, creation and salvage. I've been over this ground with her before, have talked about it with Mary till she must think I'm a broken record—Amanda and Leotis' three children—that's the creation, the objects of salvage, everything else badness. Her drinking, her indifference, Leotis' frustrated attempts at understanding what nobody can, till he gives up and spends longer than the whole days necessary tilling and planting, barn-cleaning and building, works around the clock to keep from setting foot in his own house and being rebuffed and reviled as he tries to sleep beside his witch of a wife, my daughter.

Amanda comes here sometimes mornings, smokes cigarettes, her eyes a watery gray, her underlids eroded and bagged. Always she talks about Dorie, her oldest, and always with words of love, hate, love, fear. I have to ask about Tommy and Scott and what I get is a cursory, "They're all right," dismissing them as she does Leotis, three strangers whose lives repeatedly, bewilderingly intersect hers. But not Dorie. Dorie's the reincarnation of Amanda, perfect in guile and spite, and a forlorn unquenchable desire. Dorie needs money to go to Chicago. She has told her mother, "Life is elsewhere," which Amanda believes now too. This after Amanda lied to Leotis, that the $200 she took from the account for Dorie's abortion was for new contacts. Dorie's seventeenth birthday was held listlessly from a hammock while she recovered from the previous day's ordeal. She blinked her eyes a lot as if the new lenses were not yet comfortable. For her birthday she wanted the money to go to Chicago. Amanda wonders out loud to me what should she do? Between cigarettes she worries about Dorie's future and then muses "the bitch's already buried one litter" as if Dorie killing her baby was like drowning kittens, something one does and that's the end of it. I tell her Chicago's just a big place where Dorie thinks she can hide from the small something taken from her insides and she can't, but Amanda laughs and says, "You don't know Dorie."

I say I'll pray God gives her guidance.

Amanda says, "The hell with God, who's got the money for new clothes in Chicago?"

I smack her in the face hard, my fingers burn from it, Amanda's face heats white from the blow, my prints outlined in red. She retrieves her cigarette from the floor where it's fallen and sucks in slowly, tilting her head back as if the whole world, me, were hardly worth the condescension.

"You don't know anything," she says.

That was a year ago. Dorie's in Chicago now and Amanda visits her frequently. Dories sends cash for her not to come, but Amanda spends it on plane fare. "Friends with money," Dorie says. So matter of fact that for her it's probably nothing to think about, just something you do. I ask Amanda who does she think her daughter's benefactors are. "I don't care," she says. "Except for the first few months when she had trouble getting settled, its her sending money to me. Pays for my trip and a little more, too." Her eyes blaze as if I were guilty of thinking dirty thoughts.

I involuntarily shudder and in doing so find myself again in my kitchen, a morning long started, the clock sneaking on nine o'clock and I'm an hour late for work.

It's the kind of opening Leona's looking for. "Oversleep again?" she'll ask, and cluck disapproval. What's worse is she's right. These musings on my children's and my children's children's fates hold me tighter than my own work and I sink into these thoughts as if into a dream, and I discover horribly that I have no control over myself. It's just these thoughts pouring over me. I'm a stone in the stream of them and I have no will to action, only of memory.

And then there's Luther.

I rinse out my cup, set that in the sink, scrape my uneaten eggs into a Tupperware container for Bruno, Fred and Mary's German sheperd, run some water on the plate so the remnant egg yolks aren't hardened yellow glue by the time I come back to them, and think how Luther's the first dart of life to shoot through me since little Martha was handed to me in the hospital, and even then I was one of many to whom Martha was handed, as if she were the most desired dish at a potlike supper, everyone holding her and cooing at the balled fists and pinched face (a little like Herbert when he gets upset, I thought) and then passing her on, but Luther, ah! Luther has the obstinate throb of permanence about him.

He calls me this morning, says he called the hall first and Leona said I wasn't there yet. She thought maybe I was sick, said in such a way—I can hear how she said it—she meant I wasn't.

"So how are you?"

"Just fine."

I didn't have any trouble sleeping, did I? No, did he?

"Oh, just asking," he says and I think aha! as if I were a schoolgirl.

"Well, then," he says, "I'll let you go, Leona's already in a huff," and I want to say No, wait! Tell me you had a good time last night. And as if in response to that unvoiced plea Luther clears his throat and says, "What the hell, Matty, what say we go to the Street Dance, I haven't gone in a while," and even though I was the one who did the asking first I feel the goosebumps ride over me as if I were walking in unclothed flesh on a cold, cold morning.

Leona fixes me with a look when I come in. She fixes me with a look everyday, a look of hurt and accusation that I'm still working and she can't have my job till I'm done. She'd outright run against me but knows what the outcome would be. She tried once, right after the Porter Atwood business, a campaign of whispers, and I did get less votes than when no one else wanted the job, but to most people I'm a fixture and you'd no sooner replace me with bubbleheaded Leona than you'd switch from your bathroom 60 watt bulb to track lighting. So she holds on, impatiently urging me to consider early retirement. And I probably would, too, except one of my small pleasures is watching her squirm every time she looks at a calendar.

"A good nap?"

"Has Bob dropped off the water meter numbers yet?"

"He said tomorrow, there was a lot of trash this week."

"Tomorrow's Saturday."

"Monday then. He said he'd get around to it."

Bob Synstegaard's usually getting around to rolls at Verhagen's and a soda from the broken machine at Maybolt's Garage. Spends mid-morning to noon sucking back soda, then hitches up his falling down pants and tries to get a lick of town maintenance in before quitting time. Week before trash week he's supposed to go around to everyone who didn't send in their water cards and get a reading. But he lets it slide and tries to combine the two and then forgets, and it's a week later before the numbers come in, scrawled to illegibility in a pocket notebook. "Is that a one or a seven?" I ask him and he pushes the black frame glasses up his greasy nose, the lenses blurry with fingerprints, and settles the glasses more firmly on the fleshy rounds of his cheeks, and gives me an addled grin. It's like he knows he doesn't know and that gives him an advantage.

"Well, a guy could say that was a one or a seven," he says and he grins again like my job's just been explained to me. I only ask him anymore when the number in question is in the middle or in front, where it'll actually make some difference in the bill.

"Did these already." Leona holds up a stack of yellow trifolded and stapled newsletters. Things that matter here—the quilting bee at Gert's Memorial Old Age Home, standings for the softball league (at 8-0, Borchardt Funeral Home's in first place), a reminder that lawn clippings should be double-bagged and the bags half-full or they'll split in the heat and Bob's not responsible for picking up clippings that smell like chicken shit, the fishing hours on Black Otter Lake (and no swimming since the Ott's eleven-year-old drowned), the events for the Legion's Fourth of July. All already in the *Press-Star*, but Ben Hoffmeyer's widow Alice donated $10,000 for just such a newsletter. For her, it's an extra piece of mail each month.

I look at her handiwork. "No names, no addresses."

"We'll just run them through the typewriter."

"Won't fit in the typewriter. We'll have to do them by hand."

Leona prefers it this way. She's very proud of her handwriting, a cursive full of loops and exaggerated capitals. As she goes through the address list—we have $10,000 for a newsletter into posterity and no money for mailing labels—her eyes glow, her Schaeffer pen clutched close to her bosom, which she rests on the table, and I see her imagining herself the earnest scribe in a Benedictine abbey, this transcribing a holy task.

"I'll get coffee and start at the far end."

"Could you take the A's?" she asks. "I do better with S's than G's."

"Fine," I say. "Fine, fine, fine."

"Besides," she says, "you'll get the K's then and I thought you'd want to add a note to Luther's."

I get our coffee and go to the bathroom and drink the better part of my cup sitting in there, while Leona's cup cools on the floor between my feet.

Later I'm locking up the back office when I see Luther getting out of his pickup across the street. I scoot down the hallway and into the bathroom, my hands in a dance around my head as if my straight straight brown hair could have a life different from its own. I take off my glasses and rub at the red teardrops left by the nosepiece. They're not going away so I put the glasses back on and rub at the corners of my mouth, as if a smile could be worried into existence. Then I frown and look at myself, wrinkles and all. What the hell am I doing? I march right out the bathroom and smack into Herbert, who's tried the door I just locked and is heading back out.

"Whoa!" he says, grabbing me as I stumble backwards. "I didn't see you."

"I was just getting ready to go home."

"Well, good. I've come to fetch you for dinner."

Where's Luther? Did I imagine his pickup? Herbert's taken my elbow and squires me down the hall. Doug looks up from his desk, he's reading the new copy of *Police Detective* he bought at the bottle shop, and beams approval. Later he'll go home and eat, then cruise the Commercial Club Park and later still sneak a nap in the back end of the cemetary, waiting for the bars to close when his wristwatch alarm will sound and he'll go watch for DWI's. But right now he has his *PD* and Herb's got hold of my elbow so all must be right with the world.

Do something! I want to say to him, as if Herb's interest in me in the face of my lack of interest in him were an offense worthy of arrest.

I blink in the sunlight. That is Luther's GMC, with the American flag decal by the gas cap. I look to my left, though, and it's still Herbert, determined and flateyed, his lips pulled taut in a smile more influenced by the sun's intensity than anything else. He flips down the shades that're fixed to the tops of his glasses and he looks like Jack Nicholson, only he tries to cover his bald spot with an overlong flap of hair so threadbare it looks like he's drawn brownish-black lines with a grease pencil across his head.

Luther comes around the corner.

"Luther!" I cry.

He nods hello, unsure of what to make of us, and lifts a Coast-to-Coast bag. "Run out of WD-40 and the spring-tooth's jammed."

By accident, I'm standing next to the wrong man and it's the nature of things that neither knows it. He and Herb shake hands, one of those gestures men who don't like each other insist on.

Herbert announces, "We're going to dinner."

I shake my head and gesture with my eyes: No, this is his idea. I've nothing to do with it.

Herbert says, "Well, we'd best let you get back to that spring-tooth."

"It'll keep." Luther wipes his hands on his pant leg.

We all stand, awkward, heat rising between us, Herbert earnest, blinking behind his shaded glasses, his hair junk melting down his forehead, Luther with his weight back on one foot, the WD-40 bag crinkling and uncrinkling in his hand, and me feeling so much the center of things that it's as if I were the moon and these two men moons of the moon.

In a perverse way, I like it.

Luther moves first, cutting across us to the truck with no words of goodbye and drives off. Herbert moves then, a short-legged stride, funny since he's a tall man, tossing a "Where you want to eat?" over his shoulder.

"At my house," I say and he turns to me but I cut his look short by saying, "by myself."

He nods, not surprised, and says, "See you tomorrow then," and disappears around the corner.

I go down the short sloped alley that's shaded by the fire station. Cooler here, so cool I lean my cheek into the brick and believe I could fall asleep dreaming.

Herbert's waiting by my car, having come down the other alley that runs between McHugh's Tap and Verhagen's Bakery. He stands like a true believer, hands on hood, his body tilted forward to take up space. I feel surrounded by the machinery of Augsbury—the flatbed, the backhoe, garbage truck, pickup and snowplow.

"Not without a fight," he says. "Not without a goddamn fight."

I'm thinking how calloused his hands must be, the hood shimmering heat like that. He's on the driver's side. I open the passenger door and slide across, lifting my fitted cotton dress and getting my thighs scalded. Herb's face is full in the window. I'm reminded of the Hanson's St. Bernard, jowls, teeth, watery sad eyes, the window full of him last time I came down their drive.

"Not without a fight!" In the rearview is Herbert, his fist raised in the dust.

We go out twice more. Once to a park concert I know he won't like but he's amiable about it, even holds the mosquito repellant so I don't have to keep taking it out of my purse; the other time a real dinner at Sanderson's, after which he actually kisses me. Strange, that kiss. Holding my hands in his, standing a step below me on the porch so our heads are level. I see his eyes knowing I'm waiting.

His lips were dry, wind burned. He steps back, wipes his mouth as if I'd been wearing a lot of lipstick. All I did was try to moisten his lips. My tongue heavy in my mouth like a traitor. He looks at his hand where he's wiped his mouth. Smiles. Takes an extra step so we're on the same board and kisses me proper: arms around the back, heads tilted, long intakes of breath from the sides of the mouth. The ghost of my father nods approval from the living room. Ben sighs from somewhere inside my head, the sigh he used whenever I did something I was intent on doing. I hesitate in mid-kiss, Luther doesn't notice. Now that he's committed it's like tumbling down a long hill, and then the final rush from Ben's sigh fades away and there's only Luther and I, my head full with the sound of crickets.

The next day we celebrate a long lunch at Blackie's—I take an hour and a quarter, twice my usual, and Luther's driven in with no reason, though he says he needs to make a payment at Kafka's for the spring seed.

Leona's eating her sandwich at her desk, what I usually do, and she glances from me to the clock.

"You can put what you're thinking about out of your head."

"Hard to when it's all over your face," she snaps and then righteously burrows into a ledger sheet.

I take up my work, reminding myself that giddiness, however watered and thinned by age, doesn't become us. Luther brings it up the first dinner we have at my home, where I serve him like family, in the kitchen.

"Are we something regular?" he asks, his mouth working potatoes back so the words can come out.

"I believe so," I say.

"Good," he says and continues to eat.

"Why do you ask?"

"Time I got back to a normal schedule," he says. He holds his fork like it's a pointer. "It's not like we're a couple of kids courtin'. I can't be running around paying you my respects. Least not in summer. Bunch of damn foolishness, me there on the Hill, you here, six mile drive between just to say hello."

"I've got a telephone."

"I've got nothing to say on the phone." He puts his fork down, rumples the tablecloth pushing the plate away so he can knot his hands as if he were about to pray the way men do, locking fingers, a bridge of two knotted hands, as if it were an affront to say something to God without building something first.

"Matty, why don't we get married?"

I expect him to go on, give the reasons why we should, but the question just hangs there and I almost feel obligated to list out loud why we should or shouldn't. But I don't say anything one way or the other, I just cut the pecan pie and serve it with ice cream and coffee and say, "I'll have to think." After dessert, Luther gets into his truck and instead of goodbye he says, "If we're going to the Legion Dance I'll have to learn some steps." He backs out looking over his shoulder but once on the road remembers to wave and I stand there, warm and cool inside as if two faucets were running.

I teach Luther to dance. Moving with him is like vacuuming with a 200 pound baby on your hip. He comes twice a week after evening chores and for an hour I teach him the waltz and the polka. The polka is the only dance he needs, square dancing they teach as they call it out. The waltz is for me. At weddings with Ben if I wanted to dance I had to convince other women's husbands. Ben refused to move his feet in any manner but his ambling farm walk.

"One, two, three, gliide—" I say, pushing the concrete sack of Luther's body in the direction I'm trying to go.

"Glide?" he says. "Glide?" He lifts one foot, then the other. "These don't glide."

"The polka then."

"That I can do." But I put on the Dairyland Dutchman album and all he does is hop.

"There'a no hop in a polka."

"When I learned I was taught to hop."

"I won't do a popcorn imitation just because that's what you learned in grammar school."

"Marion thought I did okay."

Marion and Ben. Sometimes I think they must've been married to each other.

I make Luther stand apart from me and I show him what a polka should look like. "Imagine there's both of us," I say, doing the double step and pause and spin and step and step and pause and spin, liking this solitary dance with Luther watching me, the music swinging into the kitchen where we've dropped the table's leaves and put it against the window and this is right I think, me dancing for myself and my husband.

Oh, I think and stop. I take a deep breath, keeping the thought far back in my head. "All right, now both of us."

"It was better just you," Luther says when we stop for the sixth or seventh time.

"But I'd look silly doing this alone at the Street Dance."

"You looked fine a minute ago."

"There are things I'll do in private that I won't in public," I tell him. This somehow says too much. We look at each other. Whoopee Norm and his Dairyland Dutchmen click off into silence.

"Again!" I say brightly, as if the idea's just hit, and I hurry to start the record over.

After three weeks Luther's passable. We'll never double polka but at least he keeps his feet moving. On the final Thursday night, the night before the Fourth, we dance like we're supposed to and then set up the table to eat. I smell our sweat mixed with the sweet odor of strawberry torte, the two smells one, achingly familiar. I can't, can't can't bring myself to say this out loud.

"What time tomorrow?" Luther asks and I tell him dinnertime.

"Okay, then," he says.

I set our plates in the sink and Luther wipes his hands on a towel and he walks to the door and out it.

"Tomorrow, then," I call.

His truck snorts alive. I go sit on the back porch, watch Fred and Mary move around their trailer home, their heads and upper bodies going from window to window, the sort of dance married people do each day without recognizing it for what it is.

Inside I dial Luther's number, the first new one committed to memory since Rupert's at the Mayo Clinic.

"Luther," I say, and he knows what I'm talking about, "yes."

I'm wearing a red dress polka-dotted white with a ruffled hem, puffed short sleeves and a scoop neck trimmed with lace. Luther's in new blue overalls and a yellow sport shirt. We look like something out of the Fleet Farm catalogue, spruced to a newness that's slightly ridiculous. Luther's starched pants legs scuff together and at every step towards the khaki and mildew-spotted beer tent already overflowing with people I feel like we're posing for a picture.

"What a pair," Og Teiken the post commander says.

"Ya, ya," Ernie Ullmer says. "They're something, aren't they?"

Ogden points. "Pies in the hall, Matty." I'd forgotten mine was in my hands, wrapped in foil. I leave Luther in the tent, go into the cave darkness of the park community hall, the dark alive with the buzz of women's voices and the giggly screechings of children. When it rains, the dance is here, two basketball hoops on each end, a pullout row of bleachers on each side, the floor worn to scoops at the doors.

"Strawberry?" Ruth Hazelton asks.

"When they're ripe, you pick 'em."

"I was hoping for one of your rhubarbs," Milly Thompson says. "When are you ever going to give me the recipe?"

"I have already, George tells me you keep getting it wrong."

"That's what he knows. I have never."

"Most people use too much sugar," I say.

"Did you hear about the Baehm girl? A second one and this time with a different father."

"Whatever happened to waiting till you get married?" Anna Schneider says. She's the only pie guardian whose neck isn't crêpey with skin. The rest are a bit lizard-like, Milly with huge glasses, Violet rhinestoned cat-eyes. They're all officers in the Women's Auxiliary. "Used to be people waited," Anna says. "Now, pow-pow, and they're not even out of high school yet." She takes my pie and puts it by the other strawberries on the counter. I see a few are store-bought, still in the box. Some women.

"Nothing's going on that hasn't always. There's only one more of them now," Ruth says.

"You only say that because you did too," Violet Tescher says.

"I never."

"How old were you?"

"Nineteen. *And* married."

"I bet you did before, everybody says so."

"Everybody says. Everybody who?"

"Joyce Kreul. She was in your class."

"She just says that because of her and Arnie before she married Roger."

"Arnie Vox? The one that died when his gravel truck tipped?"
"No, Arnie Sheepholder."
"But he's Indian."
Ruth is triumphant. "Exactly."
Violet sniffs. "Well, there's still more nowadays than before."
"All ages, too," Milly offers. She holds her glasses up toward a window and wipes them with a pocket handerkerchief. She's one of those big fleshy women whose eyes disappear, who become featureless when they take off their glasses. I know where this will go once her glasses are back on—the women of Porter Atwood. Porter's harem. The conquests of Porter. It's known he's slept with at least three women other than his wife since he got married and in one of the grandly stupid, vain and powerless moments of my life I was one of them.

It seems almost quaint now. Porter in his mid-fifties, still skinny everywhere but his belly stretched like a water-filled balloon. I can't believe it was myself or anyone else. Marion. The talk covers it all. Luther would have heard it, the names, the nods of the head. I'm chased outside, cold steel across my teeth, my head erect. Voices still going on behind me. Violet's squeaky laugh, like metal rubbing on metal. That breaks the bit, I shake it loose. It's not them, not anyone here, I have to answer to.

Luther's watching Bill and Randy Jentz throw darts. I whisper in his ear, "Let's walk someplace."

"You want a bratwurst or something?"

"Not right now."

"So where shall we walk?"

"Anywhere," I say, "I just need to feel my legs moving."

A string of firecrackers goes off not ten feet behind me. I find myself half out of my shoes and pressed to Luther's chest. A drunken laugh. Standing among the shattered bits of paper is Byron Joe Gunther, a lit punk dangling from his mouth, and behind him Herb Tessen, face pressed into a plastic beer cup. Byron Joe's shirt is open, the huge expanse of his belly pushing over his trouser tops. He takes the punk out of his mouth like it was a cigarette holder.

"Love," Byron Joe says and belches at length.

I tug Luther's arm. I can feel the cords of his forearm, the clenching and unclenching of his fist. "I won't," he says. "Not the day we're official."

I realize now why we've chosen the clothes we have: even if we look foolish, we're official.

Byron says, "Oh fuck," and lumbers off. We walk toward the bandshell. The shell's white with pea green piping and sadly needs paint. We sit on wooden folding chairs towards the back, along with the mothers with babies. They're adding chairs on stage for the concert band. Two children leap from one chair to another until their mother snatches them off.

"I should've hit him."

"It wouldn't have changed anything."

"It would've proved something."

"I'm past needing things proved to me, Luther."

"Well, I'm not. I need to know what I know." He shoots me a look, the bags under his eyes puckered. "And that matters more'n you think. You want some food now?"

Why is it a man not about to hit someone or chewing back his desire to do so isn't happy? I give in to Luther's offer and while we eat fruit Jell-O squares and potato salad and brats I ask him questions we'll need to answer: which house to live in? who gets what when we go? whose name goes where on the bank books? the titles? insurance? bills? Questions I've already answered twice, head and heart, but which Luther will have to, too, and of course he can't because any answer of his that half of me says yes to the other half will leap in with But, But—. And how do we tell our children?

"Norbert I'll send a card to, he won't come anyway. Got that rail job in Alaska, leaves in October for something in California."

"I can tell Fred and Mary this week. The rest, I suppose on the phone, except Rose. She'll be home tomorrow."

"That the one in college?"

"Yes." Rose in college, I still can't believe it.

"She gonna talk down to me or what?"

"Rose's never talked down to anyone in her life."

Luther spits. "I'm a good one to start with."

The instruments flash gold as the band takes their places. Chairs around us fill up with parents. We leave, dropping our plates in a bin near the beer tent, then walk around along by the baseball field and into the cemetery. All German and Irish, the first dated stone 1832, a girl of seven, Gretchen Marie Battenbraun. Her mother dead five years later. Grief?

"What about our houses?"

"We got two of them," he says. I pull on his hand and he says, "I suppose I thought you'd move to Mosquito Hill."

"I don't know."

"I thought you were selling what you and Ben had to Fred."

"The land, yes, and the house later, when they need it."

"Well, that's settled then."

"What would you say to driving to your place to work it and living in mine for a while?"

"What's a while?"

"How long it'll take for me to get used to another woman's kitchen."

We clear the cemetery. A block away we hear a roll of drums being tested, a trombone braying. An accordion falls out of itself. I'm afraid to live in another woman's house and I've no interest in dancing. Very faintly behind us the concert band's doing the Star Wars music. They'll close with America the Beautiful and The Star Spangled Banner, everyone singing. Then people move as a river to Main and Roosevelt and become like water frothing alongside a dam. Doug and his deputy have blocked off three sides of the intersection with two beer trucks, a holiday of white and orange sawhorses and amber lights, and the flatbed for Tony Dedoroff's Polka Princes. Luther buys us a beer to share and I drain a third of it.

"Not so fast," he says, "or I'll carry you home."

"Thirsty," I say and gulp again. People mill about, brandishing hellos. Luther keeps telling people "It's official," jerking a thumb at me and everyone says congratulations and when? And I tell them, happy but with an emptiness inside. I ask Luther to get me another beer, one just for myself and while he's gone a skyrocket goes up, one of those whistlers with a pop at the end. "My hopes," I think, and as the Princes begin with an expanding wheeze from Tony's accordion I'm reminded of the girls, the ones who come into town every night, who slug beer back fast and play pool good as a man, can roll the cue with one foot while chalking up, swear like a driver, cigarettes bobbing in the corners of their mouth, their bodies tank- or tube-topped, denim-bottomed, braless, out for all the fun they can milk from the night. This night especially when everyone's out for a whoop and a holler. Give me back two score years and my present knowledge and I'd show them something. Luther brings me my cup and I drink it too fast.

I do not want to dance.

These girls hop with each other or with their boyfriends, has no one shown them how to dance a polka? or with men who briefly, briefly catch their fancy—I think of the children who'll be conceived tonight—and they laugh and sing drunkenly and stand so their unencumbered and beautifully firm breasts stand out like prize pieces of fruit. Byron Joe pokes a meaty forefinger into one as if he were testing a rising muffin. The girl smiles and people laugh or pretend to turn the other way. I expect her to slap him, but I see now she'll make a yeasty love with him on one of the cool rounded mounds in the west end of Sleepy Oaks.

I detest and envy those who fuck in the cemetery.

Luther beams, proud to be with me (why?), also relieved we're merely on-lookers. Inside this circle couples whirl away, all ages, a true democracy, eighteen year old girls dance with their father's friends, boys with wizened grandmothers (I should talk), people married forty years or four months. Tony's singing, "I don't want her, you can have her, she's too fat for me." Women dance with women, men with men, though the men only for a single stumbling trip once around and then, laughing, they accept beer handed them by those who watch.

Marge Peterson swings by, lets go of Robert Engstrom, says, "Luther, I'll get you while you've still got a few months left," and takes him astonished into the whirling. I'm finishing my beer, watching Luther, he's got it right, though he looks perplexed, as if he were holding a child, when someone snares my hand and I'm going around, my cup splashed somewhere over my shoulder, whoever I hit steps back and laughs at himself, and then I'm pulled in tight and my eyes focus and I'm in the arms of Herb Tessen.

We dance twice around the circle, his right hand hard on my back. "So, you're up to something stupid," he says. His fingers squeeze off the circulation in my fingers. "Ssh, don't say nothin'. Just think about what you're missing." He nods as if we both know what that is. Then he lets me go and disappears. Later I see him dancing with Bonnie Elliot, a tall woman of plain face and damaged blond hair, twenty-eight or so, and they look strangely like a couple.

Luther goes past me twice more. I've already gotten another beer and Luther drinks from that.

"It's really fun," he says.

"Depends on who's your partner."

"Marge's good." He's a little out of breath. "Let me finish this and we'll go again."

"With Marge?"

He kisses my cheek. "Oh, Matty," someone calls.

Luther snaps out, "It's official," and kisses me again, this time on the mouth. We must be drunk. I close my eyes. Applause. I imagine the wedding: Mary shushing the fidgeting Martha with a stage-whispered, "Quiet, Grandma's getting married." The two of us emerging from the church in a rice kernel rain, a vintage tractor and buggy with iron spoke wheels and skinny rubber tires waiting to chauffer us through Augsbury's streets, over the bridge Luther's son drove off, we won't be able to not think about that, but still we'll be happy, and to many waves and a few tears and loud jokes about the night ahead we'll be driven off to settle into whoever's house we end up choosing.

I do not want to dance.

But we do. An energy greater than mine moves me around, I think of orbiting moons and this time don't like the comparison. We're sweating. I'm too aware of my shrunken body inside the polka-dotted dress that sticks to my stomach and back, the puff gone out of the sleeves. Luther wears the thin smile that tells people he really does like this. I've drawn him out after too long without anyone and he shines like his life finally again means something.

Tony Dederoff winds up with "In Heaven There Is No Beer," and thinking the words in my head I forgot myself. A party, this is a party for everyone. Then Tony announces that after the break there'll be more dancing, square and polka, till the highway has to be reopened at midnight. The band bounces off stage and over Black Otter Lake the fireworks start. A quick burst of three to get everyone's attention, and then single ones, one after another so everyone can ooh and aah, recite their awe like prayers.

My arms and legs tingle, especially the upper reaches of my thighs. This is as much as I will get and I ask Luther if he very much wants to keep dancing.

"No, I don't have to," he says and I ask if he'd mind taking me home, I want to leave before anyone notices and in saying goodnight to people they won't let us leave.

Luther gets his truck. I meet him on the near side of the beer truck, where there's only Og Teiken. "Going so soon?" he asks.

"My foot bothers me a bit." I shift my weight and extend an ankle. Og nods. "You see she gets home safe now, Luther."

I say, "Goodnight, Ogden. And thanks."

"We do what we can, Matty. It's a goddamn great country, isn't it?"

We repeat goodnights and Luther and Ogden shake hands. But then he doesn't drive me home. Instead he turns up the sandy double-rutted road of Sleeping Oaks. Winds to the very back where the bright aluminum painted steel legs of Augsbury's water tower are splayed like a reluctant beast. Luther shuts off the lights and puts his right hand on the back of the seat and slides over from under the steering wheel. I hear the engine ticking heat. His first kiss is gentle, lips nibbling just in front of my ear. Then both our mouths, hard, searching. My head snaps back. He kisses below my chin.

"Luther?"

His breath heavy on my neck. "Isn't this what you wanted?"

Yes, I want to say, want to breathe it out of me, but No is threaded through the syllable. Can the two slide into each other? Not possible, nothing like it possible, yet my skin prickles where he kisses me.

A wire runs through my arms. Not me, but yes. One hand touches Luther's chest, the other reaches down and opens the cab door. I lead us under the crossed girders of the water tank. High above us it's like another planet, the nest of the tower dark and silver, the sky exploding away to the left.

We fuck like two old dogs. I don't want to see his face. His hands fumble, trying to get inside the front of my dress, my skirt hiked. I'm glad it's dark so he can't see the skin gone toneless, the legs like old sausages hung up to age. My palms and knees spread my body's shuddering into the earth. The body absorbs, the earth abides. Then the reverse. I want to sing a hymn to the beauty of this perversion. I want to pray: Please, God, understand this is the nature of things, that we do what we know will displease You, that our sins are sometimes good.

I can't fathom the contradiction and I'm too caught up by the pleasure to stop. I move in the rhythm of Luther's grunted ahs, feel them taking over me, my pulse one beat from his and then we're going in tandem, yes and yes and yes and then Luther's rough hands works through the bunched cloth, masters the fabric gone unruly in passion, reaches me and rubs and soon after his pumping stops with a long groan and sigh I collapse forward into the ground shuddering, shuddering and still.

I roll over. Luther's on his back, his overalls wormed down around his knees. His penis has shrunk and looks ill-used, lost in a lathered tangle of hair. He's asleep. I wake him and we dress, not looking at each other. At home I put our clothes in the hamper and tell him to shower before he comes to bed. I take a basin bath with a washcloth and soap, gingerly around my privates. I try to sleep, held by Luther, who's out again almost before his head hits the pillow. The faucet drips in the bathroom and I get up to turn it off, then walk to the front of the house. The GMC glows brown in the driveway. I think of hiding it, driving it into the shed, but then think, No, the mercury light on it is better. I go to bed, Luther moving to give me room. I sleep, dreaming of the children we will not have.

I get up at six and outside where I looked last night the word "whore" in runny letters of whitewash has been painted on Luther's truck. I throw on a robe and with my heart furious in my chest, call Herbert and read him the riot act.

"How dare you paint such a thing on Luther's truck!"

"Put Luther on, Matty. I've got to 'range a time with him." He sounds drunk.

"Don't be stupid."

"You know well as I the right thing often 'pears stupid to people."

"Getting your face broken over nothing *would* be stupid."

"Nothing, is it? You sleep with a man and you call it nothing? Luther know that? Luther know you think that? That word's on his truck for his benefit, too."

"Luther's not going to fight you. I'm going to scrub that word off and make ourselves a breakfast and he's not even going to know what you've done, is that clear?"

"Tell 'im behind the Kafka Feed Mill at eleven tonight. Won't nobody be around and we can square 'counts."

"He won't be there, Herbert. This isn't Gunsmoke, for God's sake—what do you think? I'll sigh and say, My hero! Is that what you're hoping for? A lucky punch and life with me forever?"

"Just let me talk with him. Let me tell him the kind of woman he's getting."

"Dry out, Herbert."

"Whore," he says and hangs up. That's as far as it'll go. Herbert's strength of character stops somewhere between skulking around at night with a paintbrush and outright action.

But there's still the mess on the car. I run some hot water and still in my nightie, my robe falling loose about me, I scrub and scrub till the word goes away. Only there's still the outline, as though the rest of the finish faded ever so slightly overnight and sunlight strangely makes the ghosts stand out. Luther doesn't notice, though I feel it's embossed on the side of his truck. By the time he's up I've gotten clothes on and eggs are snapping. I jab with a fork, breaking yolks.

Rose and the friend who drove her arrive mid-morning, Rose on her crutches, the friend sporting long, tan legs she moves as if they were her only limbs. Luther left after breakfast, wearing a too-small pair of Ben's pants. Too hot to use the dryer, I've washed our things and hung them on the line outside. Rose's friend is Susie, several years younger but then they all are. Rose worked at the toy factory for several years, pulling a lever that stamped human features into wooden gingerbread dolls. That money and a disability scholarship got her into college. Susie is one of those thin and hungry-looking women so often attracted to knob-jointed Rose. I wonder if they think of it as a sort of penance, a mortification to spend time with her, noblesse oblige of the shapely. I suspect anyone who befriends Rose, afraid their motive is pity. But we have a nice lunch talking about the summer and school, both work in the library, and their plans for a winter trip to Florida. "Where the boys are," Susie giggles, as if she's given herself away. They're on their way to Wheaton, Susie's home, for a long weekend. After lunch she plops herself down in front of the TV for a soap. Rose and I sit out back.

"Whose overalls?" Rose asks.

"Would you believe me if I said Luther Krake's?"

"With the two crazy sons?"

"I wouldn't say crazy."

Rose's tongue appears at the corner of her mouth. "Seriously, who?"

"Seriously, Luther Krake."

"Does he sleep here?"

"That's none of your business."

"But does he?"

"I like him."

"I haven't gone to bed with the men I've liked."

Rose is twenty-nine. I try to imagine her—a crooked version of myself, same elliptical face, straw flat hair, freckles, green eyes, same tight muscular frame, except for the bulbous joints and gnarled fingers—in bed with anyone.

Rose sips lemonade. "What do Fred and Mary say?"

"I haven't told them."

"But they know."

"Mary seems to think it's all right."

"So do I. Just don't marry the bastard till you're sure you want to."

"We already have a date."

"That's no reason."

"I didn't say it was. Anyway, how about you?"

"Well, I'm not thinking of getting married anytime soon." She smiles, her capped front tooth a bit in front of the other. That's what remains with me when they drive away: a smile that connects us.

Luther eats with his usual appetite. I just watch. When he finishes he says, "Let's go to bed."

"Just like that?"

"I've got chores. I'll smell later." He holds his mug out for more coffee.

"I'm not a cow that needs milking, Luther."

"Jesus, woman, I just thought—"

"What? That after Porter—"

"You said it."

"It's on your tongue."

"Well, what was last night? Pretty much abandon, wasn't it?" He grabs my arm. "Wasn't it? Wasn't it just like with Porter? Marion'd back you up on that. Only she had the sense to get him while he was young—"

I'm beating on his shoulders. Then the blows are on his face. My little finger gets gashed on his teeth. Blood comes out his nose. He's still got my one hand held and is trying to catch the other but I swing away and the hand lands again, this time with a resounding crack! His nose makes the sound ice does when you put it in a hand towel to break it and he lets go of me and I stand away and say, "Jesus God, Luther, what did you expect?"

His head's tilted, blood running into his ears, his kerchief pressed to stop the flow. From under the cloth he says, "I wanted to see if you would."

"Get out of my house."

"Just let this stop, will you?"

"I'll get some ice."

The ice turns his nose red and purple and the blood's stopped. With gauze and white adhesive tape I make a tent to cover the damage. Luther stares at the ceiling.

"I had to know if I was just another one," he says. "Otherwise, how else could I marry you?"

"We're not getting married."

"Because I had to know?"

"Because you confuse me and Marion and think I do the same. I was stupid once and you think I repeat stupidities."

"Women do."

"Fuck you, Luther Krake."

Luther dismisses my anger with a wave of his hand. "You can't tell me we were going to get married for love. The only things different now are I know I'm not Porter and you broke my nose."

"What's different is I don't want to get married."

"I still want to sleep with you, Matty."

Too much silence. Then something painful. "I still do, too."

There's something about Luther, the way he walks from the bathroom, penis stiff with expectation, that makes him look like a wind-up toy. Later, he's asleep and I put my robe on over my nightie and make a pot of Lipton's, sitting in the dark kitchen to drink it, hugging myself and gently rocking.

Luther is for myself, I think. I run a town's business that would probably run whether anyone saw to it or not and I've worried about my children as they drift off like so much dandelion fluff. I keep accounts of their lives now as if my heart were a city ledger. Credits: Isabel with a good job for herself and married (an executive for Winona Knitting Mills), now trying to get pregnant after years of fearing she would. Rose will be a librarian. Fred and Mary will have my house, work the land and raise Martha and the others to come after. Debits: Matthew and his family too far away, too busy to visit. Amanda. Falling off the cliff of herself, Leotis paralyzed, watching the fall. Frankie—Texas or Arizona. I've stopped thinking of Frankie as being anything but gone, kept alive inside me as Ben and Rupert are. These last four years a slough, work I do because it's work, children I can only keep superficial track of as the duties of their lives take them out of mine. I count children as beads on a rosary, going from one to the next, connected but barely to the others, as if I were getting somewhere.

I never got what I prayed for on the rosary, either.

That's not entirely true. After Ben I prayed not to feel alone. I thought Rose would stay. Instead God sent Herb Tessen and Luther. It would be too much to call it love, and Luther's fire is sometimes stoked by another woman's name, but I have the warmth of satisfaction within me, a satisfaction I'll have to see Father Reardon about, if only to explain why I do what I do. Bless me, Father, for I will sin.

False dawn now, the sky blurred into the ground, gray sky and green trees still identical. Later I'll sit in Mary's tiny kitchen, tell her how I cannot marry the man I'll sleep with, and later still, she'll explain to Fred. A cock crows, fooled by the lightening sky and I wonder how it'll be over at Luther's, those nights I'll stay there. I worry about the mornings most, trying to get used to a kitchen I don't know, where the cupboards won't be where they're supposed to and there's no plants and the window probably faces stupidly to the north. I take out coffee from the fridge and rinse the pot, then fill it to the ten cup mark. While that's going, I go back to Luther and sit on the bed. I run my finger along the taped damage of the nose I've broken. Luther opens an eye halfway and says with disbelieving knowledge, the word nasal through clots of blood, "Matty?"

I nod, nervous for both of us.

C. J. Hribal was born in Chicago and raised in Wisconsin. After receiving an M.A. in creative writing from Syracuse University, he taught there until 1983. He currently lives in Minneapolis with his wife, Krystyna Hribal-Kornilowicz, their dog, and an assortment of dying plants. He is now working on a novel. *Matty's Heart* is his first collection of stories.

THE MINNESOTA VOICES PROJECT

1981

\# 1   Deborah Keenan, HOUSEHOLD WOUNDS (poems), $3.00

\# 2   John Minczeski, THE RECONSTRUCTION OF LIGHT (poems), $3.00

The First Annual Competition

\# 3   John Solensten, THE HERON DANCER (stories), $5.00

\# 4   Madelon Sprengnether Gohlke, THE NORMAL HEART (poems), $3.00

\# 5   Ruth Roston, I LIVE IN THE WATCHMAKERS' TOWN (poems), $3.00

\# 6   Laurie Taylor, CHANGING THE PAST (poems), $3.00

1982

\# 7   Alvaro Cardona-Hine, WHEN I WAS A FATHER (a poetic memoir), $4.00

The Second Annual Competition

\# 8   Richard Broderick, NIGHT SALE (stories), $5.00

\# 9   Katherine Carlson, CASUALTIES (stories), $5.00

\#10   Sharon Chmielarz, DIFFERENT ARRANGEMENTS (poems), $3.00

\#11   Yvette Nelson, WE'LL COME WHEN IT RAINS (poems), $3.00

1983

\#12   Madelon Sprengnether, RIVERS, STORIES, HOUSES, DREAMS (familiar essays,) $4.00

\#13   Wendy Parrish, BLENHEIM PALACE (poems), $3.00

The Third Annual Competition

\#14   Perry Glasser, SUSPICIOUS ORIGINS (short stories), $6.00

\#15   Marisha Chamberlain, POWERS (poems), $3.50

\#16   Michael Moos, MORNING WINDOWS (poems), $3.50

\#17   Mark Vinz, THE WEIRD KID (prose poems), $3.50

#18 Neal Bowers, THE GOLF BALL DIVER (poems), $3.50

Jonis Agee, and others, eds. BORDER CROSSINGS: A MINNESOTA VOICES PROJECT READER, $8.00

The Fourth Annual Competition

#19 Margaret Hasse, STARS ABOVE, STARS BELOW (poems), $3.50

#20 C. J. Hribal, MATTY'S HEART (short stories) $6.00

#21 Sheryle Noethe, THE DESCENT OF HEAVEN OVER THE LAKE (poems), $3.50

#22 Monica Ochtrup, WHAT I CANNOT SAY/I WILL SAY (poems) $3.50

Copies of any or all of these books may be purchased directly from the publisher by filling out the coupons below and mailing it, together with a check for the correct amount and $1.00 per order for postage and handling, to:

New Rivers Press
1602 Selby Ave.
St. Paul, MN 55104

Please send me the following books: _____

_____

_____

_____

_____

_____

I am enclosing $_____ (which includes $1.00 for postage and handling)
Please send these books as soon as possible to:

NAME _____

ADDRESS _____

CITY & STATE _____

ZIP _____